LUCK

Stories

Ed Meek

TAILWINDS PRESS

Tailwinds Press
P.O. Box 2283, Radio City Station
New York, NY 10101-2283
www.tailwindspress.com

Published in the United States of America
ISBN: 978-0-9967175-8-8
1st ed. 2017

CONTENTS

To Elizabeth

LUCK

PART ONE

THE ORCHARD

The light those cool fall mornings would slip surreptitiously into our damp tent. Caroline and I had our sleeping bags zipped together to form a rectangle. I would wake up tangled in her hair, my lips pressed against her neck. I loved the taste of her skin—salt and sweat, and the feel of her skin—down and silk over smooth stone of bone. I'd turn and squint at the shaft of light, motes suspended, drops of dew, and yank myself up to get dressed. She'd take her sweet time so I'd leave first and head over to the common fire Burton would have raging, the smell of coffee percolating in the tin pot.

There were four of us camped out for the harvest on the orchard that fall. Lizzie and Burton were in a teepee. It was 1976. The teepee was made of canvas. Lizzie had bought it at L.L. Bean. She said she always wanted to live in a teepee and this was her chance. The orchard was owned by a guy that Burton knew. Burton was Lizzie's boyfriend. He had gotten the owner to hire Lizzie,

Caroline and me. Lizzie was Caroline's sister. Lizzie and Caroline, along with a handful of migrant women, graded and packed apples. A dozen male migrant workers picked the apples.

Burton and I did everything else—picking up the apple crates and loading them onto a flatbed behind a tractor, unloading and stacking the crates in the barn, loading the graded, packed boxes of apples onto trucks, repairing any of the variety of jeeps, pick-ups, tractors, and farm equipment necessary to keep the operation moving, and making apples into cider using an old manual press in the barn, loading the gallons and half-gallons of cider onto the bed of the pick-up and delivering the jugs to local markets. We worked six days a week. And on Sundays Caroline, Lizzie, Burton and I sold apples and cider at the farm stand. In the afternoon, one of us would go food shopping for the week's supplies.

Every morning the four of us would rise at dawn, have coffee and bread or muffins for breakfast, and we'd work till noon when we'd break for lunches of tomato and cheese sandwiches and cider; then we'd work until dusk when we'd gather at the farmhouse for dinners—home-made hearty soups, brown rice and fresh vegetables. We'd take turns making dinner. On Sundays, roast turkey and potatoes and beans cooked by the owner's wife at the house in town were ferried out to the farmhouse for us.

There was always a rush of one kind or another—to pick the apples before the frost, to pack the apples and ship them to make room for what hadn't been picked, to press the apples into cider before they went bad, to stock for the weekend, to fix whatever had broken down—hard work—twelve, thirteen hours a day, nearly all of it against nature's backdrop—undeniably beautiful in its array of color, marking each day the changes in birch, maple, oak and elm—from pine-needle-green, to sun-splashed yellow to cranberry to maroon to tangerine, all of it repeating again and again in waves of color that rolled into hills and mountains that stretched one behind the other, backing up the story of nature the trees had to tell, a cacophony of color, a kaleidoscope of time.

That September afternoon I was sitting on the back of the flatbed. The flatbed was attached to a tractor. Burton was driving the tractor between the rows of apple trees. I would hop off and load the boxes, filled with apples by the pickers, onto the flatbed. It was hot and sunny. I was sweating right onto the apples. I liked using my body, working hard in the heat. I had always liked it hot and sunny. Most summers I'd spent on the beach on Cape Cod. There, I'd work at night as a bartender and go to the beach during the day, but I had been going out with Caroline at school since winter and when she asked me if

I wanted to work on an orchard in July and August I figured, why not?

Caroline and I had both graduated from Emerson College in June. We were supposed to be looking for jobs. The plan was to work on the orchard for two months, but I had convinced Caroline to stay on and now it was almost October. We both had degrees in Art. September was a good time to look for jobs down in Boston. By the end of the harvest, most of the good jobs would be gone. But we were a long ways from Boston. Much farther than the three hours it took to get there from New Hampshire by car. We were in another world.

Burton pulled the tractor up to the barn and shut the engine down. I started unloading the boxes and stacking them inside the barn.

"Hey," Burton said, "what's the rush?" He smiled. Burton was never in a hurry. He was a lanky dude with long hair he kept in a ponytail that came out the hole in the back of his green John Deere hat. He was laid back, cultured in the wisdom of his years. He was much older than us. He was almost thirty.

"What are you gonna do after the harvest?" I asked.

Burton leaned against the boxes. "Lizzie and me will go back to Novie. I have a place on the ocean up there. Thinking of getting a boat and starting lobster fishing in the spring. Already got some pots. Usually in the winter though, I do carpentry. Done some work as a mechanic too. I can always find something."

I grabbed an apple from a box and bit into it. The sweet citrus juice and the tart aftertaste twisted my tongue. Burton picked up an apple, took a bite then threw it at a tree and missed. Burton and Lizzie had met in a pub in Nova Scotia. Lizzie and Caroline were from Wellesley, a tony suburb of Boston but they had grandparents up in Nova Scotia and Lizzie had worked as a waitress and lived up there for the last two years—since she graduated from high school. She and Burton had met in the spring and Burton had told Lizzie about this orchard he had worked on for the last couple of summers. Lizzie told Caroline and Caroline told me.

"You missed," I said to Burton. "You never miss." Burton was a capable guy. He could fix all of the equipment. He seemed to just know how to do things, how machines worked. A tractor would stall and he'd fiddle with the engine and the engine would turn over. There were a lot of people like that when you got out in the country. People who knew how things worked and how to fix them when they broke. People who knew how to build houses. What did I know? How to make drinks. How to catch a ball. How to seduce women. How to create paintings even I didn't understand. Could I spend the winter in New Hampshire or Nova Scotia with Caroline? I'd bartend and she'd waitress. Maybe I could work as a laborer or train as a mechanic. I had already learned a lot from Burton about fixing jeeps and tractors. I didn't want to go back down to Boston and bartend and paint on the side. That was Lizzie's plan—work in restaurants and do art on the side. Like Burton said, what was the rush?

Caroline and Lizzie were grading the apples in the basement of the barn. They'd pluck the apples from the crates and place them in boxes according to how they looked. If they were perfect and shaped just right, they would go in one box; if they had slight imperfections, bug bites or sunspots, they would go in another. If they were seriously flawed or misshapen, they would go into a bin for cider. When the boxes were filled, they'd be closed and stacked. What Caroline complained about first was the chafing of the cardboard box against her wrist when she placed the apples in the squares formed by cardboard dividers. By September she had developed a rash on her wrist and red scrapes lined her arms. Caroline said she could never get comfortable—the migrant women kept the windows open because they would all sweat, where Caroline was cold from drafts of air. She said it was always damp in the barn basement. Her back would be cold but the sleeves of her shirt would cling to the sweat on her arms. She and Lizzie worked alongside migrants who had come from other harvests out west. The migrants, their husbands and their children, all stayed in the bunkhouse. They spoke Spanish to one another, ignoring Caroline and Lizzie. Their kids played just outside the barn during the day.

One September afternoon, Lizzie came strolling out of the barn. Maybe she had heard Burton and me or maybe she just wanted to take a break. "It's a hundred degrees in there," she said. She pulled her jersey off. She wasn't wearing anything underneath. She patted her face, her breasts and under her arms. I noticed the hair under her arms was blond. Her skin was the color of peaches. I couldn't help but stare. I looked at Burton to see how he was reacting.

"Hey," he said to Lizzie, "keep your shirt on!" He laughed.

"Who cares?" Lizzie said. "You don't care, do you David?" She pulled her jersey back on and walked back into the barn.

"No," I said, "not me."

That night I found myself restlessly tossing. Caroline had already told me she hated living in the tent. It didn't really bother me. I was pretty happy working hard all day and by nightfall, I was so tired I could have slept anywhere. But it bothered her that we would only get to shower on weekends in the bunkhouse where the migrants slept.

Caroline said sleeping in the tent made her feel ugly and dirty. I rolled over and put my hand on Caroline's arm despite the fact that she had let me know that the last thing she wanted was to be touched. She claimed that season she was learning to just say no. If things had been different I might have been angry but I was so wiped out by the end of each day that I would usually just conk at night. I figured we'd get back to normal after the harvest.

Anyway, Caroline was asleep with her back to me. I moved closer to snuggle. I kissed and nuzzled her neck. I had one hand on her leg. I pressed up against her from behind. It felt good. I thought I heard her murmur with pleasure. I was picturing Lizzie without her shirt on. She had beautiful breasts. Her skin was pale and smooth. She was thinner than Caroline but her breasts were bigger.

All of a sudden Caroline jabbed me in the ribs with her elbow. "David, I was asleep. You were humping me while I was asleep. What are you, a dog?"

"I'm sorry," I said. I couldn't really make her out in the darkness. "I didn't know what I was doing. I was half-asleep myself; I thought you were sort of awake."

"Sort of awake?" She rubbed her elbow and began crying.

I didn't know what to make of Caroline's tears. "I just wanted to make love," I said. "I wasn't forcing myself on you."

"That's exactly what you were doing." She wiped the tears away with her jersey.

"Ugh," she said, "you are disgusting. I hate this place and this awful tent. I want to take a hot bath."

I reached around for the flashlight. I kept it right next to the sleeping bag, but it must have gotten knocked away.

"I want to quit," she said. "I want to leave here, tomorrow, or the day after, or this weekend, before I completely lose it."

"You were the one who wanted to come here," I said.

"I know, but now I want to leave and go back to Boston and find a good job. God, it doesn't even have to be a good job. Anything, as long as I can go home at night and take a hot shower, sleep in a bed and wear clean clothes in the morning. And I want to get back to painting. Don't you miss it?"

"It's so beautiful up here, I don't. I'm not even sure I want to paint anymore." I felt suddenly exhausted. I lay back and covered my eyes with my arm. "Let's talk about this tomorrow," I said. I rolled over and drifted to sleep dreaming of Lizzie.

When I woke up in the morning, Caroline was already up and out of the tent. I tried to get my thoughts together. I could just let her go on down to Boston and join her in a few weeks, after the harvest. Or I could quit too and leave with her. Part of me knew that if I let her go, that would be it between us. On the other hand, if I left with her and we cleaned up and went out in Boston (there was a restaurant I could take her to in the North End—a place she loved), I thought I could turn her around and we could get back on track again. The weird thing was that as I was arguing this with myself the image of Lizzie kept insinuating itself into my thoughts. I was really kind of angry at Lizzie for doing what she did. Taking her shirt off like that in front of me. What was she doing anyway? Was she being competitive with her sister? Was she flirting with me? Because if she was, it had worked. She had hooked me. She had one-upped her sister there and then. I suddenly wondered if I really loved Caroline. I couldn't really love her if just the sight of Lizzie without her shirt on could distract me so much.

When I got to the campfire, Caroline was drinking coffee, talking with Burton and Lizzie. "I told them I'm leaving," she said to me.

I could see that she was giving me an ultimatum. It was leave with her or else...

I poured myself some coffee. "I'll stay until the end of the season," I said. I was saying it in part just to gauge her reaction but when it came out, it sounded right to me.

"Well, I'm out of here today," Caroline said. She wouldn't even look at me. "I'm going to pack and then I'll find out if I can catch a bus in town."

"David and I can drop you off when we do the cider run," Burton said.

I watched Caroline walk back to the tent. She had definitely gained some weight. I was trying to figure out how I had ever found her attractive.

"By the way," Burton said to me, "you're welcome to come with Lizzie and me to Nova Scotia when we're done here. I can hook you up with some work and you can stay with us."

I smiled and looked at Lizzie. I wondered what the rest of her body was like. I was trying to play it out in my head—how it might go up there in Nova Scotia. Would Burton kill me if I stole Lizzie from him? He just might. He could peg me with a knife in my back from fifty feet. They'd find me face down in the snow. One thing was certain, it would get ugly, but maybe it would be worth it. I sighed and looked at the trees. "Let me think about," I said.

I was checking out the foliage. The leaves had turned burnt orange and blood red. I suddenly shivered. There'd be a frost soon.

NARCISSUS

Kelly had come to Boston to get back together with her boyfriend who, it happened, was my new roommate, a guy who referred to me as his best friend. His name was Sam. Sam was one of those idealists out to educate the poor. He taught history to kids who didn't believe in history in a middle school in Boston.

We became friends because I had recently moved into a two bedroom apartment in Boston and I was looking for someone to share the rent. Sam answered my ad and moved in. Sam had moved from his parents' house on Long Island when he got the teaching job in Boston that fall. Before he moved in with me he had been staying at the Lenox Hotel. He'd been there for a month.

Sam stood about 5' 6". He weighed in at 145. In high school he had been a wrestler. He had long hair and a beard. He wore jeans and sneakers to work. He held his head up and he tended to stick out his lower lip. His eyebrows met above his nose.

He had a lot of albums—rock, jazz, classical stuff, but what he seemed to listen to most was that mainstream folk music that was popular at the time—Jackson Brown, Joni Mitchell, the Eagles, Neil Young. I liked that music, but every time I'd put on one of those albums Sam would take it as some kind of approbation or something. He seemed to think we were soulmates since we were living together and liked the same music. He liked to roll his eyes at me. I would talk to him about politics and history. I learned a long time ago that if you ask people questions, they'll gladly talk and if you're interested, they'll enjoy talking to you. I'm always interested in hearing people talk about whatever it is that they like or know a lot about. Sam seemed to take this personally. Don't get me wrong, I liked Sam. I just didn't think of him as my best friend.

The way Sam saw it I had done him a favor, finding him a place. Whatever duties we had to share, he did a little extra, whether it involved cleaning, shopping, cooking, you name it. Sam would do the dishes, clean the floor, run out to Stop & Shop to pick up some bread and cold cuts for a late night snack. He even made an extra copy of his car keys and gave them to me. He drove a '68 Ford Mustang with a V8. I didn't have a car at that time. I had owned a Honda Civic but I sold it when I moved in town because I figured in town I wouldn't need a car. I took the subway to work and everything I wanted to go to was within walking distance of my apartment. But Sam insisted I take his car if I went out on a date, or if I wanted to drive somewhere on my own. Like Ruth in the Bible, I was taken in—part of the family.

I remember this one time. I had borrowed Sam's car to drive over to Harvard Square. I sometimes went there to go to a couple of bookstores I liked: WordsWorth and the Kiosk. WordsWorth was a great place to pick up paperbacks and to browse through the new stuff, and the Kiosk had just about every magazine and journal you could ask for. I liked to buy an occasional *American Poetry Review* or a *Ploughshares* and the Kiosk was a good place to get the small literary magazines. Plus you could stroll down to the Coffee Connection or the Algiers and get an espresso and look at the artists and revolutionaries who hung out at those places.

So I had just come back from Cambridge, I was hungry and I knew there wasn't much to eat in the fridge. I walked in and there was Sam with a big spread on the table: fresh tomatoes, a hunk of New York cheddar and a huge jar of mustard. He had been waiting for me.

"I got the mustard today," he said, "Kelly sent it from France."

It was one of those mason jars filled with Dijon. Not the Dijon you get in the little jars, this stuff was strong, creamy and aromatic. Sam had a round loaf of Italian bread hot out of the ovens of Bova's bakery across the street and we made up a couple of oversized sandwiches with the tomato and cheddar and mustard. He had bought a four-pack of Whitbread Ale. It was the first time I drank it and I don't believe there's a better brew in the world. It's big and rich with a body that won't quit.

Sam handed me one and said, "Enjoy."

The guy seemed so happy I just had to smile.

"Not too shabby," I said when I had taken a bite and chased it with the English ale. And things really weren't so bad right then. With the money from Sam I was able to pay the rent and I could see that Sam was a pretty nice guy. I hoped everything would work out with his girlfriend. She was coming in from France the next day and Sam and I were going to pick her up. They had been apart for the six months she had spent overseas. Some people seem to weather these separations better than others. Sam had expressed anxiety about seeing her again after the long time apart.

I was more than a little relieved I didn't find Kelly attractive when Sam and I picked her up at Logan Airport. She looked like a cheerleader from Ohio State. She had blond hair she wore in braids. Her eyes were blue and they twinkled when she smiled. She had a wide mouth and her smile seemed to light up her face. Her skin was a little blotchy. I think she was worn out from the trip. She had on jeans and a peasant blouse and she looked like she had enjoyed the French food. Sam had mentioned that she said in her letters she had gained some weight.

The reason I was relieved about not being attracted to Kelly was that I hadn't always been what you would call trustworthy around women. One of my high school chums had an older brother who was a real lady killer. One of those cool, tough guys who always seemed to be angry about something; he would fight at the drop of a hat. I didn't like him so I went out with his girlfriends. I mean, I didn't just go out with them because I didn't like him. The girls, Paula and Karen, were both nice in their own right. I would have gone out with them even if they weren't going with Mark. But the fact that they were just added another dimension. Mark ended up marrying Paula and later divorcing her. The other girl pined for him for years. I didn't win their hearts. I just went out with them a few times.

And the reason I wasn't attracted to a girl who looked like a cheerleader from Ohio State was because I looked like the captain of the baseball team. Not at Ohio State. More like UMass. That's where I went. And I *was* the captain of the baseball team. What I mean is I was your run-of-the-mill half-decent looking Irish-American guy. Six feet tall, well built, sandy hair, hazel eyes, friendly smile. The last person I was attracted to was the cheer-leader type. I went for exotic looks. Extremes. Girls with dark hair and dark eyes. Girls with hair down to their waist or hair so short it was fuzzy to touch. Girls with hair bleached white blond. Girls six feet tall. Someone who didn't look even remotely like any of the women in my family. Why? I don't know. Maybe I was still rebelling, working out the old Oedipal thing. Admit it though, how many times do you see these couples who have really gone out of their way to find someone completely the opposite of them physically? Think back to your first relationships, or even your first marriage. Weren't you gone on someone your parents wouldn't dream of fixing you up with? And doesn't it make you puke to see these couples who look exactly like one another? Remember Mick and Bianca?

Well, Kelly was going to stay, at least for awhile, in our apartment. According to Sam, he and Kelly had one of those on-again off-again affairs. They had met at Kenyon College. After they graduated, Kelly decided she needed some time to herself. That's why she went to France while Sam returned to Boston to teach.

It was OK with me if she moved in with us. Hey, no problem. It was 1979! We were all still living under the aegis of the sixties—"Let it be," sang Paul. Plenty of room. Nice to have a woman around. Did I mention there were no doors on the bedrooms? There had once been doors but they had apparently been removed. The holes for the hinges had been painted over, probably when the apartment had been renovated. It was an old apartment in a brick building that held five units. Wide-board wooden floors, dropped ceilings. Big, curved bay windows over-looked the street. There were the two bedrooms, a small living room and a big kitchen with a dining area. Sam and I furnished the place with odds and ends from relatives and from sales: an overstuffed couch from his grand-mother, chairs from my aunt, an oak dining table we found at a used furniture store, a yellow Formica kitchen table I found in my parents' basement, folding chairs from my uncle. The bedrooms had plywood walls. The ceiling in the kitchen had a hole in it and occasionally plaster would fall down on the floor. The area for the dining table was in an alcove with the bay windows. We could eat breakfast or lunch there and look out at the action.

I slept on a futon on the floor of my room and Sam had a waterbed in his room. The first night that Kelly was there I was lying in my futon reading about some lovable psychopath in a Jim Thompson mystery and I looked up to see Kelly scampering past my door in the buff. It was like a vision: pale white skin and long blond hair seen out of the corner of my eye. I fell asleep dreaming of angels.

Welcome to the Hotel California—"This could be heaven or this could be hell," as the Eagles sang. No doors with two guys doesn't really matter much, but no doors with a woman in the place is a problem. Sam and Kelly tacked up some of those beads fortune tellers use. Lot of good that did. The second night I listened to them make love. He came first and then a couple of minutes later I heard her high-pitched sighs. I got up, got dressed and went down the street to the Caffé Pompei for a cappuccino with a shot of sambuca.

The next day all three of us went shopping at Haymarket. Haymarket is a farmer's market which is set up on the streets between Faneuil Hall and the North End. The vendors sell produce mostly: lettuce, spinach, cukes, tomatoes, and fruit—oranges, grapefruit, lemons, limes, bananas, strawberries, mangos, figs—whatever is in season somewhere in the world. The vendors are all competing against one another and they sell this stuff by the box. If you go to Haymarket you don't spend much and you come home with more than you can possibly eat.

So there we were, looking over the bargains and Kelly was all lit up. "Woah!" she said, smiling, "this is great stuff." She couldn't get over the variety and how cheap everything was. She stopped at the stand with the juice oranges. They were selling four dozen for a dollar.

"How about five dozen for a dollar?" She looked at the vendor and smiled. He was a guy, fifty years old, skinny as a rail with four days growth. A cigarette dangled from his mouth. He wore a rumpled fishing hat and a dingy white tee shirt. What I knew from shopping here for a couple of years was you don't bargain with these guys so I waited for the guy to snap at her.

"For you," he said, "five dozen for a dollar." He loaded the oranges in a bag and handed them to Kelly who put them in a cardboard box that I got to carry since I was the big guy of the group.

"Nice work," I said to her. It was a sunny day in October and the sun played off her long, blond hair. When she smiled her blue eyes sparkled and I found myself smiling back.

She bargained with everyone. We ended up with two boxes of fruit and vegetables. Sam had one and I had the other. On top of mine was an array of squashes: spaghetti, pumpkin, acorn. Sam had strawberries, blueberries, raspberries, blackberries, bananas and a big pineapple.

I hoisted the box up onto my shoulder and held it with one hand and we wound our way back through the narrow streets to the apartment. We stopped at the small brick bakery run by nuns and bought a twist of fresh baked bread. At the grocery on the corner Kelly bought a liter of extra virgin olive oil. "From Lucca," she said. She bought colossal Greek olives, a half pound of feta cheese and a soppressata sausage. Outside she made us wait while she dashed across the wine store and picked up a bottle of red wine.

"They had just what I was looking for," she said to Sam. She took the bottle out and held it up for us to see as we walked up Salem Street.

"Chianti?" Sam gave me the eye.

I shrugged my shoulders. I didn't know much about wine.

"Ah, yes," Kelly said, "but it's an Antinori Chianti Classico."

In the apartment we sat at the dining room table with our feet up. The big, wide curved windows were thrown open. The sun sent spokes of light into the room. On the mahogany table sat the half finished bottle of chianti. We ripped hunks of fresh bread off the twist and sesame seeds scattered on the table top. Sam cut slices of soppressata, a dry-cured sausage, and we put it on the bread with pieces of feta.

"Not a bad day's work," Sam said.

"*Pas mal*," Kelly said.

"Good wine," I tossed in.

"What makes you say that?" Kelly said with a sly smile on her face.

"Come on, Kelly," Sam said.

She laughed. "I'm just asking a simple question."

"Well," I said, "it's lighter than chianti usually is. It doesn't have that inky taste, and it leaves a dry aftertaste in your mouth."

Kelly turned her mouth down and nodded her head. "Not bad," she said to Sam. "Not bad," she said to me.

It struck me that I had passed some sort of arcane test.

Meanwhile Sam and Kelly started right off quibbling.

"I need more space," Kelly said.

Sam nodded sympathetically.

I got up and went to my room, but I could still hear them.

"If I can get some work then I could afford my own apartment," Kelly said.

"Wait a minute," Sam said. "I thought we were going to try to stick together. Try to work on this."

"I don't know, Sam, I guess I've gotten used to sleeping in my own room, making my own decisions." She lowered her voice to a whisper: "Plus, I'm just not comfortable in this situation."

"I know," Sam said. "But, we'll work it out."

I was a bartender. One of my college roommates, Steve Gillis, managed a place called, get this, Narcissus. He had some family connections with some shady characters. The bar he managed was owned by the mob. I knew that. But Gillis and I had worked together in restaurants while in college doing everything from cooking to waiting and bartending. So when I got out and the job market was tight, I decided to go to work for my pal.

The year before, the place had actually been called Lucifer's, I swear it's true, but they changed the name to Narcissus just when I started working there. I guess that was how the owner, Henry Vara, saw the difference between the seventies and the eighties and you know, he wasn't so far off. In the seventies we did indulge a bit. Norman Mailer said: the devil is shit. He meant drinking and drugs, junk food and TV and schlock magazines, and bad art, one night stands, sex for its own sake, sex for the sake of lust. And as Henry Fairlie said, lust isn't picky. Erich Fromm says love is an act of will but Fairlie says lust is a will-less act. Did I say will-less? Does that word have three l's in a row? Those three l's are the erections of young American males who watch TV and movies, who stare at the covers of the fashion magazines and who read *Playboy* and *Penthouse* and stand on street corners watching women parade by like ducks in a row to be picked off or picked up and toyed with and cast aside until another girl comes along.

And the Eagles were onto something too: heaven, or hell, could be either. It's all jumbled up here in America. We really don't know. According to a national poll most people believe in heaven, but few believe in hell. And since the Catholic church closed purgatory we're pretty much set, aren't we? We can do no wrong. Richard Nixon was really a pretty nice guy once you got to know him and so is William Jefferson Clinton. Bill just seems like a megalomaniac. He's actually charming and ah, boyish. I'm sure he didn't actually take any bribes from foreigners for bedrooms and I think we all know what he means when he says he never had sexual relations with Monica. Meanwhile, as Dan Quayle might have said, our family structure is a wreck on the sea of life; our values are fish washed ashore and left out in the sun to rot.

Though the name had changed, Narcissus still had the garish red walls and high, tinsel ceilings with three bars—two on the first floor and one on the second with a balcony overlooking the dance floor. The dance floor was raised and colored lights revolved above the dancers. There were twenty or thirty little cocktail tables, big enough to hold drinks. The waitresses wore white blouses and short black skirts. When Henry Vara changed the name of the nightclub, he added mirrors. Mirrors everywhere—behind the bar, on the walls, on square posts in the middle of the floor. You couldn't get away from yourself in that joint.

On weekends the place was packed by 10 p.m. with secretaries, college kids, foreign students, and working class kids. Sometime around one o'clock, a few gangsters would stroll in and take up residence, backs to the wall, behind the front bar near the door. That way they could keep an eye out.

There was a register for each bartender on each bar. That way management could keep track of what you were doing. Gillis worked me in as the third bartender at the front bar. I wouldn't even go to work until about 10 p.m. Yet I would get a full cut of the tips we pooled. It would come to around a hundred. Naturally the other bartenders resented me. I was Gillis' pal, where they had all worked their way up to bartending in Narcissus by working first in the owner's other, less glamorous clubs (Henry Vara owned half a dozen places). I had walked in off the street and been put right on the front bar.

So I'd breeze into that nether world of Narcissus and don my black bow tie and slip into the front bar and make drinks as fast as I could get the sticky six ounce glasses filled with ice and whatever combinations of booze and juice the crowd asked for. Screwdrivers, gin and tonics, Seven and Sevens, margaritas, greyhounds, salty dogs, golden dreams, mai tais, Budweiser, Miller Lite, Heineken. I worked as hard and fast as I could while B.B. King played "Lucille" or Harold Melvin sang "The Love I Lost" or Evelyn "Champagne" King belted out "I Will Survive." They had those name acts on weekends. And the dance floor was filled with students from B.U. and secretaries from the North Shore and late at night, the gangsters would file in. You could tell they were gangsters because they acted tough, were overly polite, pulled out great wads of cash from which they paid for their drinks and left swell tips. They wore flashy suits, had gold teeth, and they talked tough.

"Yo, give me and my good friends here a round. You know me, right? What are you new here? What's your name? It? Id? Ed! Oh, Eddie, OK, look I'll have a scotch rocks—Johnny Walker Black, same for Red, right Red? Give Henry a scotch and milk for his ulcer, give Bobo a

Heineken and give those two girls over there whatever they're drinkin. How much is that?"

The guy I'm thinking of was Frankie Damato. He used to come in all the time. Like everyone else he worked for the Angiulos, who were running things back then. This was before the FBI sting that broke up their power and put the old man away. His son Jason would drop in on Saturday nights. Jason was about my age and for a gangster, he was very smooth. Jason had gone to college, studied business and returned home to help dad out with the business. The business involved owning half of the waterfront property in the North End, a couple of liquor stores, the High Hat strip joint in the Combat Zone, the numbers racket and a loan shark operation in the North End, the South End, and the North Shore, and a stolen car ring which they ran in conjunction with the Patriarca family out of Providence, Rhode Island. Jason was always very quiet. He would come in with two bodyguards. If anyone stared at Jason for too long or brushed past him, the bodyguards would put their hands in their sport coats on their guns, but nothing ever happened to cause them to draw their weapons when I was working.

Anyway, I had only worked there a couple of weeks when Kelly asked me if they needed any waitresses. I didn't think she was the waitress type but you never know, right? I asked Gillis and he said, "Sure, we're always looking for waitresses."

The next week when I came in, Kelly was there, lined up at the end of the bar for drinks and carrying the little circular trays to the Middle Eastern students and the secretaries and the working class white kids. And you know something, she looked pretty good in that little black skirt and white blouse with her long, blond hair and her big smile. She had lost about ten pounds since she'd been back. Of course the lighting in Narcissus wasn't great, and those little skirts and the black fishnet stockings the girls wore, well, they all looked pretty good. Still, she didn't look like the same person I had met two months before at the airport. I couldn't figure it out to tell you the truth.

So, we became pals. She would take Sam's Mustang to work. I would take the train over because, as I said, I didn't go on until much later. Then after work she would wait for me while I cashed out and we would drive back to the North End. The first few times we went straight home, but I'll tell you something, when you work in a nightclub, especially a busy place, you run, you work hard and the people you serve, they work your nerves. They spill drinks, they want something other than what they ordered, they're out to pick you up, whatever. By the time you're through, you're nerved up—a little on edge and the only way to get to sleep is to have a couple of drinks and wind down so you go to some joint that's open a little later than the rest and you have a couple of Stolys on the rocks.

The guys I worked with had a whole routine after hours. The owner of Narcissus, Henry Vara, also owned the Two O'Clock Lounge in the Combat Zone. The guys would go down there and drink, do drugs, fool around with the strippers. Then they would wander out of the Combat Zone as the sky in the east began to brighten.

Anyway Kelly and I would stop at the Caffé Pompei, which was right down the street from where we lived. You could have a cappuccino and a drink there. The cops didn't bother the place because it was owned by the Angiulos. It was a typical Italian café with an espresso bar in the front, a gigantic copper espresso machine, a glass case full of pastries and cakes, and behind the pastries a cooler with homemade gelato—Italian ice cream. Behind the copper espresso machine were bottles of sambuca, strega, vodka, gin and scotch.

Frankie Damato would always be there. He was friendly to me. He came over to the table where Kelly and I were sitting and pulled up a chair, turned it around and sat with his arms over the back. He had a toothpick in his mouth and his gold teeth gleamed.

"Hiya kids," he said. "Yous two go out together?"

"Well, not really," Kelly said, smiling.

"Not really? Not really?" Frankie turned to me. "I like that. She says not really. That's cute. You two make a nice couple. Let me get you a drink. You're always gettin me drinks, right Eddie? Let me buy you a drink." He turned and motioned to one of the guys behind the bar.

"So, Eddie," he said to me. "Could you use a Cadillac? White? The works. I'll give to you for, ah, let me see, ah, five grand. You can't beat that. This thing has 1100 miles on it. What do you say?"

"No thanks," I said. "I don't need a car."

"Don't need a car? I offer you a deal like that and that's all you have to say?" Frankie shook his head and looked at the floor. "I thought you was smarter than that, Eddie, I really did." He looked at Kelly. "Will you talk to him? Talk some sense to him? You seem like a smart young lady." Frankie got up. Our drinks arrived and Frankie pulled out the wad of cash he kept rolled in an elastic. He peeled a ten off the top and threw it on the table. "Think about it," he said and headed towards the back room of the café. The back room, separated by curtains, was where the gangsters hung out. They usually had a card game going back there. At least that's what I had heard from the other bartenders. I had never actually been back there myself.

After he had left Kelly said, "He's kind of intense."

"Hard guy to say no to," I said.

"Would you buy a car from him?" she asked.

"No, no way. All those other guys that work at Narcissus drive them though. Bobby has that '57 T-bird that Frankie sold him. Bobby thought it might be a little too visible but Frankie told him it was from Florida and not to worry. And John got his Caddy from Frankie. I guess Gillis must have gotten his car from him too; he drives a Lincoln."

"You trust this Gillis?"

"I really don't know," I said. I hadn't really thought about it, but I guessed I didn't entirely trust my old pal Gillis.

"So," I said, "do you like it there? At the club I mean?"

She looked at me over her cappuccino into which she had just emptied a shot of sambuca. "Yea," she said. "It's kind of fun. And it, ah, gets me out of the house."

"It's a kick for me, but I can't feature doing it forever."

"What I mean," she said, "it's nice to get away from Sam." She stared at me to make sure I had gotten the message.

I sat back and thought for a few seconds. I could just let it go. These days I would, but back then I was always game. I wanted to know things. "What do you mean by that?" I asked.

"It just isn't working out," she said. "I go into that apartment and I feel like I'm stuck on an island with Sam and he's not the guy I would choose to be stuck on an island with."

"What are you gonna do?" I asked.

"Well I have to save some money. Eventually I'll find my own place."

It was late. I paid the check and we walked home. We didn't say anything else that night.

Sunday morning I dragged myself out of bed at ten. Sam and Kelly were arguing. He wanted to take a day trip, make a lunch, have a picnic even though it was December.

"I'm tired," Kelly said. "I worked last night."

"And you didn't come home after work, did you?"

"No, I had a drink with Ed."

"You say you were with Ed, but maybe it was someone else. How would I know?" Sam's voice took on a whining quality during these arguments.

"Ask Ed," said Kelly, "he's right there." She pointed to me.

"She was with me," I said in as deep a voice as I could muster. I tried to make light of the situation.

"I don't believe you," Sam said. "You're taking her side."

I didn't know what to say because although he was wrong about Kelly being out with someone else, there was truth to what he was saying and he must have sensed it. I *was* taking her side. At the same time, I thought he was being silly and I began to wonder what she saw in him. I still liked him well enough. He was nice to me, but I didn't get their relationship. I decided to chalk it up to one of those things I didn't understand about women. Who could figure why they got involved with one man instead of another. You saw them all the time on the street, in restaurants, in nightclubs—beautiful, intelligent women with gnomes, deadbeats, drudges. Some were easy to figure—they had just taken the best deal they could get—the house and the car and the expense allowance. It didn't seem to matter to them that they had to actually sleep with the guy for twenty years. That didn't seem to be a consideration. They didn't seem to care that they actually had to look at this guy's face across the breakfast table every morning for the rest of their lives. They didn't think about what the children would look like and be like. They were just on the arm of some pushy salesman who wouldn't take no for an answer. But Kelly and Sam weren't in that category, were they? No, this was one of those rebellious relationships. They were rebelling against mommy and daddy.

In Sam's case his folks wanted nothing more than a nice Jewish girl who would pass on his name and their religion and culture, and Kelly's parents? Kelly's parents wanted nothing more than a nice WASP with whom she would have blond babies who would be brought up as Christians. Nothing more than that she marry some honest, decent guy who would work in insurance like her father had and who would provide her with a house in the suburbs. But they had gone to college in the seventies and they were still feeling the aftershock of the sixties and that meant that they did what they wanted to—their own thing. They had to find themselves after all, didn't they?

"Maybe I should pick you up after work," Sam said. "Then I won't have to worry about you."

"That's it," Kelly said, "I'm moving out!" She stomped into their room and would, I'm sure, have slammed the door had there been one. Since there wasn't, she dashed the beads against the wall. One of the strings broke and a couple hundred beads scattered on the floor. She sat down on the waterbed and put her face in her hands and cried.

Sam looked at me. He had that hang-dog look on his face. The ends of his mouth turned down and his big, brown eyes were just about ready to gush. It was pathetic all right.

I shrugged as sympathetically as I could. I looked at the beads on the floor and I looked back at Sam. Then I got down on my hands and knees and began picking up the beads.

"Oh, shit," Sam said, turned around and walked out leaving the door to the hall open. Well, I thought, I'm just going to pick up these beads and then, let's see, there were some things I wanted to do—a little shopping. What was it that we needed? Coffee? Bread? Cheese? I'd have to make a list. I looked up from the floor into Sam's room. It had gotten quiet in there.

Kelly was lying on the bed looking at me. She was smiling slightly. I glanced around the floor. I had most of the multi-colored beads in my hands. I stood up and dropped the beads into the trash can we kept under the sink. I turned and started to walk out the door. I was trying not to look in Sam's room, but I couldn't help it. My eyes drifted over that way and there she was—still smiling, lying there with her back to the wall in her blue silk bathrobe. I stopped. She drew one of her legs up and put her hands around her knees.

"Going out?" she asked. She put her hands behind her head and leaned back. There it was—the soft white inside of her thigh set off against the deep blue of her robe. I stood there and tried to keep my eyes on her face but there was no helping it. I followed the line of her robe right down to her leg. I was sure she noticed and it only seemed to make her smile more.

Ladies, what can I say, we men are weak in such circumstances. Show us your legs, or the tops of your breasts, the outline of your fanny, we're in trouble. We're ready to do whatever we, in our libido-crazed imaginations, think you want us to do.

"I thought I'd run out to the store," I said. I stepped forward and, pushing the beadless string aside, walked into the room. "Is there anything you need?" I bit my lip. "The lower lip of desire," Neruda called it.

She got up out of the bed and went to her bureau. "Let me give you some money," she said.

Okay, I could still go, is what I was thinking. Walk right out the door. No problem. She hesitated at the bureau. There was a mirror above it and she looked into it, first at herself and then at me. I was there in the mirror too. My eyes wide open and ready. I began to feel a physical ache for her. It was almost as if I were leaning toward her, about to fall. She turned on her heel and walked up to me with the money in her hand. She put the bill in the front pocket of my jeans and I got hold of her hand and pulled her toward me.

Hey, you know it's true: men are wired for sex. Go way back, fifty, a hundred thousand years—we're wired for the survival of the species. Women are only fertile a dozen times a year. We have to try and try again. And what are we attracted to, today, one hundred thousand years later? Those areas of the female anatomy associated with reproduction—the breasts, the buttocks, the legs that lead inevitably to the fertile crescent.

So Kelly and I made love that Sunday. While others went to the church of their choice we remained, like John Lennon and Yoko, in bed. If heaven is a state of bliss then we were in heaven. We made love all day while Sam was out, who knows where.

So, I was thinking, Sam and Kelly got together because they were the exact opposite of everything their parents were and wanted. It was fun until they realized that that wasn't much of a reason to stay together. Now we kissed, necked, smooched and caressed. We gave each other the massage of our dreams. Maybe it was exciting in part because of the tension of Sam's presence; it was being naughty and getting away with something. And there were other sources of tension. For the past few months we had been attracted to one another although we hadn't really been entirely aware of it. We had refused to admit it, even to ourselves. So we went along, day to day as if nothing was out of the ordinary and that Sunday it was as if the floodgates had been opened and we rode the white waters of sex, hour after hour. Perhaps we also thought we might not get the chance to be together soon again and so we had to keep making love as if it was the first and the last time for both of us.

For me it was like coming home. The smell and texture of her skin and her hair are what made me dizzy. Smell, that undervalued sense, so important when we roamed the savanna, today relegated to the austere position of enjoying rare meals, fine wines, the flowers of spring, and the mounting piles of waste and garbage we're leaving for our descendants to clean up. Yet smell is so basic to us—what does the mother do first when she draws her infant to her but deeply inhale the baby's scent. And before the child can even see, he smells the scent particular to his mother. We may cover ourselves with deodorants and hairsprays, and perfumes, but beneath those covers there is a smell and it is that smell that you must love. If you turn from kissing your lover's neck when she wakes in the morning, beware.

Now her mouth which at first seemed too large was just right—full, sensuous lips I couldn't get enough of. And long with love though that Sunday was, Sam failed to return and foil our romance. He stayed away until nightfall, by which time we had risen and bathed and returned to our respective rooms. I finally did go out to the store to pick up those staples and Kelly turned to her diary to do some writing.

I remember that trip to the store. You know the feeling—walking on air. That and every other cliché you can think of. We all fall into the realm of cliché when we fall in love. Eskimos used to say that falling in love was a form of madness. They were right. Crazy in love is the phrase. I suddenly loved the North End. Those punks on the street weren't bad kids at all. Those bag men on the corner were really pretty swell guys when you came down to it. And I was on my way to pick up some fresh bread, and the wholesome products we take for granted in this great country of ours—the milk and cheese, and vegetables we pick up for a mere pittance. It's kind of ridiculous really, the way we are at such times.

And although I was waltzing down the street like Fred Astaire, I was also troubled in the back of my mind. I knew I had betrayed Sam, who thought of me as his best friend. I rationalized it by saying that they were finished as a couple anyway—he and Kelly, and was it my fault that we had fallen for one another—it was bigger than both of us, wasn't it? Well, we would just have to confront Sam with the truth and play it out no matter how bad it sounded.

So that night we sat down to break bread together and after a sumptuous meal of pasta and homemade tomato sauce with basil and oregano and olive oil from Lucca, after a bottle of barolo that was so big and rich, it was a meal in itself, didn't Kelly and I sit opposite Sam and confess our love to him? No, I'm ashamed to say. We did not. We joked around as if nothing had happened.

"That was a wine and a half," I said.

"A mighty big wine," Kelly said imitating John Wayne. She walked pigeon-toed to the sink.

Sam shook his head and laughed. "You two," he said. "What would I do without you?"

Kelly and I looked at each other expecting the worst.

"Maybe I just needed a little time to myself," Sam said. "I took a long walk today—across the river to Cambridge. I went to an old movie called, I think, *Trouble in Paradise.* It was directed by Ernst Lubitsch. Made in 1932. I didn't know any of the actors or actresses in the movie."

I had actually seen it. "I loved that movie," I said.

"It was almost like *Twelfth Night*," Sam said. "Everyone in love with someone else, conning each other and loving it, having a swell time."

"I like it at the end," I said, "when the leading man says to the woman he's just stolen a necklace from, 'It would have been marvelous, darling.' And she says, 'Yes, darling, it would have been marvelous.' And he goes off with the other woman. It was great."

"Only in the movies," Sam said.

We sat around for awhile and then Sam and Kelly went into their room and turned out the light. Now, it was my turn to go for a walk. A group of half a dozen Italian kids were hanging on the corner as usual. They were a little boisterous this evening. Two of them seemed to be having some kind of argument. They were practically spitting words at each other. I had a hard time understanding what they were saying at first so I sat down on my stoop across the street to listen.

"You don't want to mess with me," a young, dark-haired kid was saying. He looked about twenty to me. He had on a black leather jacket, worn open, and underneath, a tee shirt. It was about 38 degrees out and there was a chilly wind blowing off the Atlantic.

"Joey, look, Joey, I'm talking to you. I'm trying to talk to you." This was an older guy. Definitely the oldest guy in the group. He must have been 45. The rest of them were under 21. He had a big knit sweater on and glasses pushed back on his head. His hair was gray and cut short. He had his arms folded. "Joey," he went on, "I'm just giving you a message. Telling you for your own good. This stuff has got to stop. Two a dem gone, three a yous. Where's it gonna end?"

I suddenly realized they were talking about the Fleet Street murders. There had been five murders committed in the last six months and apparently these guys were the other gang involved. Fleet Street was three blocks away on the other side of the main street that ran through the North End.

"Joey, you know how it is. We don't give a shit, normally, what you do long as you don't interfere with our business, but all this trouble is bringing the heat in. Not the cops. Them we can handle. The politicians. Outsiders."

For some reason he looked over at me when he said that. I just got up and walked away.

"Who was that?" the older guy said.

"I think he lives in Sal's building," Joey said.

An outsider, that's what I was. What Sam and Kelly and I all were—outsiders. We had moved into a small, tightly knit neighborhood which consisted almost entirely of Italians. Well, they would just have to get used to us because the neighborhood was changing, wasn't it?

That night I walked up over the hill past the old North Church which stood stark white against the sky and on down Charter to Atlantic Ave. I turned right and walked past Lewis Wharf where the Angulos had leased the land to put up waterfront condos. When they were finished and sold those buildings to professionals, the North End would be even smaller, hemmed in by the rich who would eventually supplant them altogether. I walked up to Columbus Park to look out at the bay and decide what to do. There were a couple of kids with long hair swimming. They must have been drunk. One of the most polluted harbors in the world and they were out in it at night. A cop strolled over to the fence which separated the land from the water. He peered down the six foot drop into the darkness. He looked over at me and shook his head.

"I ain't goin in there," he said to me. He called out. "Come on outta there."

The two kids turned out to be a guy and his girlfriend who were visiting from Ohio. They both had long hair and nearly identical outfits of jeans and denim shirts. Her hair was red. They were laughing when they climbed out of the water. They must have been really loaded.

The cop talked into his walkie talkie and within a couple of minutes a cruiser pulled up. A sergeant climbed out from behind the wheel. I walked away as they put the offenders into the back seat of the police car. The two cops were arguing about whether to bring them to City Hospital or to the Holiday Inn in Kenmore Square.

Well, much as I hate to admit, nothing changed for the three of us for a while. Kelly and I got together when we could. The rest of the time we were all good pals. Until one night a few weeks later when Kelly and I were working. It was, I believe, a Thursday. It was slow and Kelly was done early. In bars if it's slow, management sends you home. Just one of the ways they save a few bucks. When we weren't working, we could get drinks half price so we'd usually hang around a while and down a couple. Bobby and John had closed down their registers and they were sitting at the back bar with Kelly.

Kelly walked over to the front bar where I was working. It was only about 11:00 and I wouldn't be done for a couple of hours. "I was going to take the train home," she said, "but Bobby said he'd give me a ride."

I looked over at Bobby and he winked at me.

"You all right?" I asked Kelly.

"I took a Quaalude," she said, smiling.

Bobby came over. "I'll get her home, Eddie," he said.

I had to serve a few drinks so that was the last I saw of them. I was a little worried. Sure, Kelly was a big girl but she had finished a couple of drinks and a lude. Ludes made you loose. Loose and feeling good—things could get a little wild.

Two hours later I finished up my shift and drove straight back to the North End. When I got there the door was open and Kelly was in the bedroom crying. Sam was gone. It looked like he had taken some of his stuff.

I didn't say anything. I figured they had argued it out and he had split. I took off my clothes, climbed in bed and we made love. Afterwards she told me what had happened.

"They fucked me."

"What?" I didn't get it at first.

"Bobby and John," she said. "In the back seat of John's Cadillac. I was really loaded. I was practically passed out in the back and I just didn't have the energy to fight off Bobby. He did it first. Then they switched places and Johnny did it. He didn't come. He wasn't even hard."

I got up out of bed. I had a pack of cigarettes in my room that someone had left on the bar and even though I didn't smoke, I lit one up. I couldn't believe what she was telling me. I kept looking at her to see if she was the same person I thought she was. I suddenly felt really uncomfortable. Like I had been in a line to do sex with Kelly. "Why didn't you tell me before?" I asked. "Doesn't that make me number three?" I lit a new cigarette off the one that had burned down. I went out to the kitchen and poured myself half a glass of Jack Daniels—neat. "Did you and Sam do it before I got here?"

She was sobbing now. "No," she said. "I told him what happened and he left. He said he's going to take a leave of absence and go back home to New York." She reached out to me. "Please lie down," she said. "Hold me."

I drank the bourbon, put out the cigarette and lay down on the bed. I held her.

Sam never even came back. He called me from the train station. His voice was cracking as he spoke. "I can't believe it," he said. "I need a little time to get things together."

He told me he'd call from home and let me know what he was going to do.

Maybe I should have walked out too. Or maybe I should have forgiven her, realized she'd made a mistake. If she were a guy, what then? No big deal, right? Or maybe she was just like those kids from Ohio who'd jumped in the harbor for a swim—she was loaded and didn't know what she was doing. But, I don't know. It changed the way I looked at her. And it bothered me that she didn't tell me right away when I got home instead of waiting until afterwards. That just made me feel like I'd been part of an orgy. I didn't like the feeling. But I didn't desert her. It just cast a pall over everything.

She quit her job as waitress. Three weeks later she caught a lucky break and picked up a job as a secretary at WGBH. It was a weird situation for me at work. As far as those guys knew, they were OK with me because Kelly was not my girl. I had told all of them she was going with Sam. Still, they were uncomfortable with me. I gave my notice and picked up another bartending job almost right away at a club across town. Kelly and I saw each other less and less and finally not at all. Today you might call what happened to Kelly date rape. Today I'd be worried about AIDS. Back then it was different.

THE FALL OF IRAN

I spent two years in Iran—from 1977-1979. When I arrived, there were over fifty thousand Americans. Two years later nearly all of us had left. In 1977, the Shah was firmly entrenched in power. By 1979, he was fleeing the country to save his skin. I went with my girlfriend Kelly. We rented a house in *Taj Rish*—a village on the northern fringe of Tehran. Soon after we moved in, I remember sitting in our landlord's living room on his Persian carpets. Pillows and short-legged tables were the only furniture. We were drinking tea.

"Very good—*Kube*," Kelly said, pointing to the tea.

The landlord's wife went into the kitchen and returned with a box of the tea leaves from which the tea we were drinking had been made. She smiled and presented the tea to Kelly. We had cake with the tea and Kelly made it known in the little Persian she knew that the cake was delicious. The landlord's wife went to the kitchen and brought the rest of the cake in a cake tin and gave it to us to bring home. We said, "No, we couldn't." But she insisted.

Later, as we were leaving, Kelly told the landlord that she thought the carpet in the living room was beautiful. The landlord looked suddenly stricken. He turned to his wife who shrugged. Then he said to us, "Please, I want you to take it."

"No," I said. "We couldn't."

"Please," he said. "I insist."

"No," I said. "It's impossible."

"I want you to have it," he said.

I shook my head. "No."

He mopped the sweat from his brow with a handkerchief and smiled weakly.

It was only later that I learned that if a guest says he likes something, the Persian custom is to offer it to the guest. The host must make the offer three times. It is only if the guest refuses three times that the host is off the hook. That tells you something about the survival of tradition in Iran, and something about the graciousness of the host—the idea that whatever he has is yours.

The house Kelly and I rented was built into the mountains. Not fifty yards away the minarets of a mosque cut into the sky. Five times a day a mullah sang his praises to Allah and the rocks seemed to affirm his faith with their echoes. We were happy then. At least, I thought we were happy. We had come to Iran together to get away from the U.S. There was so much going on in America; things moved so quickly that we thought if we came to Iran together we could figure things out. We weren't entirely sure whether we wanted to stay together. The change of scenery seemed to work. Where I had been plagued by doubt in the U.S., in Iran, I could see that I loved Kelly. I thought that all I needed was to get away from home to gain some perspective. When we went back, it was clear that Kelly and I would get married.

In Iran it appeared as if things had been the same forever; Iran was, despite modernization, fundamentally unchanging. Yet by the fall of 1978, a year later, Kelly and I, and my landlord's son Ali, were standing on the roof of the house Kelly and I rented, having a beer, and watching for the flashes of light when the Shah's British-made Chieftain tanks fired off rounds aimed at anti-government forces. A moment after the flash, we'd hear an explosion. The Shah's troops were attempting to contain the opposition who occupied much of the old southern section of the city.

In less than a year, Iran had gone from a peaceful country, controlled by the firm hand of the Shah, to a nation torn by civil war. There had been talk on the streets and in the papers since we'd arrived about the West exploiting Iran for its oil and the Shah being in the pocket of the United States. There was an anti-government protest at a movie theatre in Tehran in September of 1977 just after we arrived. A number of students were arrested and the general feeling was that the Shah was in control. But during the following year, things slowly got worse and worse with more protests by students. Then the clergy got behind the students and you could feel a seismic shift in the culture. By the fall of 1978, Americans working in Iran began to question just how long the Shah would last.

Now Ali, our landlord's son, was talking to Kelly and me about deserting from the army. There had been more protesting by Iranian students and many of them had been shot down in the street. It was a beautiful warm night in December. We were standing on the roof, drinking German beer, watching the fireworks.

"The Iranian Army shouldn't kill Iranians," Ali said. Ali was on a two-day leave that weekend, but instead of reporting back, he was talking of heading north that night with his uncle to stay in his cousin's summer house on the Caspian Sea.

It was hard to tell that December of 1978 just what the Iranian Army would do. The Shah had declared martial law and President Carter had pledged his support, but these soldiers were the descendants of the forces of Xerxes who, 2,500 years ago, had ruled over the Persian Empire. When a storm made crossing the Hellespont impossible, Xerxes is said to have ordered his troops to whip it into submission. Whether they were successful or not depends on whether you're talking to the Greeks or the Persians. Persians will tell you they subdued the waters of the Hellespont and won the war against the Greeks and only withdrew from Greece out of benevolence. Most Persians are Shiite Muslims who believe the spirit of Mohammed lives on today and speaks through the mullahs. As mystics, they think history is open to interpretation, and time moves in circles rather than a straight line. The Persian Empire was said by the mullahs to be returning from the ashes of history. And Persians have a long memory.

Kelly had a job as a secretary for Bell Helicopter, but business was at a standstill and Bell was already offering to fly any American employees home for free.

"What do you think I should do?" Ali said to us.

"I think you should desert," Kelly said.

"I don't know," I said. "You have to make that decision Ali."

Kelly glared at me.

"Maybe you should take off, Kelly," I said, finishing the can of Becks. "Return to America, I mean."

"No way," Kelly insisted. "If I stay until March of next year I get my $5000 end-of-contract bonus."

"I have to go. *Khoda-afez*," Ali said to us, shaking my hand. He climbed down the ladder to the roof and headed across the courtyard to his father's house.

I was a teacher at Iranzamin International School. In fact, the other reason I had come to Iran was that there were jobs. Unlike most other Americans though, I wasn't exactly making a fortune. I was paid about 20K. Kelly was making much more as a secretary. Engineers were making piles of dough. I wasn't there for the money. I was interested in seeing a different culture and being there with Kelly. It seemed like a unique opportunity and really, it had been easy. I answered an advertisement in the *Boston Globe*, went to an interview and a couple of months later I was on a plane to the Middle East. The school paid for my ticket. I paid for Kelly's with money I had saved bartending in Boston, and she paid me back shortly after she picked up the job at Bell.

By Christmas of 1978 work had slowed down at Bell. Meanwhile, I was on Christmas vacation. We didn't know if school would open back up again after winter break. Around that time I began to have the feeling that Kelly was distancing herself from me. I thought if we did something together, we could have some fun and maybe get a chance to talk.

Kelly and I hooked up with our friends Janet, John, and Carmel. We piled in my car to go skiing in the mountains north of Tehran. That day we were heading down what was then Shahanshahar Avenue and what is now, no doubt, Khomeini Drive, when a soldier directed me onto a detour. The detour turned out to be a sheet of ice descending at about five degrees. We slid slowly down the road. I pumped the brakes and the car turned sideways. All my companions were laughing and shrieking. Like a boat coming into a dock in a storm, we plowed into a parked car, making an accordion dent in its door.

Cars were still new to that part of the world and Iranians drove them like toys. When an accident occurred, and they occurred often, crowds gathered. Hardly anyone in Iran had auto insurance so, when Iranians had a car accident, particularly a minor one, they would argue endlessly about who was at fault. The crowd would join in and eventually, the case would be settled, right then, on the spot. An accident with a *farengi*, or foreigner, could be profitable to Iranians who were rumored to crash into Americans to make a profit from the devils exploiting their country.

The Iranian who owned the parked car came out of his house. He must have heard all the noise. A crowd of Iranians began to gather, arguing about what had happened. I offered the owner of the car I had hit my insurance card and told him the company would settle in full. He took it happily, assuming he would get more money than if he bargained with me then. The crowd, disappointed, dispersed. We pushed my car back onto a dry patch of road and took off. Whether the insurance company would actually settle or not, I didn't know. I suspected their money was frozen. But I had lived through two years of being overcharged by cab drivers, rug merchants, fruit sellers, and butchers. I had spent two years doling out bribes to everyone from train conductors to ensure I got the seat I was supposed to get, to mailmen to ensure I received the mail that had been sent to me. I had had enough.

"Is that insurance card any good?" Kelly asked.

"Hey," I said, "there's no way I'm going to pay for his damages. It was the soldiers' fault sending us onto the ice and if the insurance company doesn't pay him, that will be a little payback for me for all the *baksheesh* I've been handing out since I've been here."

"Damn straight," Carmel said.

"That doesn't make it right," Kelly said.

Halfway to the ski resort we got a flat tire. While I was changing the tire, I noticed a demonstration going on in a nearby village. I was almost done when the crowd spotted our car and with shouts of *Magh Ba Emrica,* Death to America, they began marching towards us. I spun those little nuts in place, tossed the tire iron in the trunk and jumped into the front seat while rocks clattered on the roof and in the road around us. As we squealed out I could see the Iranians running in the rearview, chanting and shaking their fists.

"That was close," Janet said as we drove off. She had been walking home from the market the week before when some kids, shouting anti-American slogans, had thrown rocks at her. Janet was an administrative assistant for Bell Helicopter. She weighed in at about ninety pounds and her recently acquired heroin habit was making it hard to keep the weight on.

"You must be joking," Carmel said. "That wasn't close at all."

Carmel was Australian. She was a reporter for the English newspaper in Tehran. She loved a little danger. Carmel was tall and thin with long, wavy brown hair. She was attractive but her aggressiveness seemed to keep her leaning forward all the time, jutting her chin out, ever ready with a derisive comment.

Once we were at the ski resort, everything was fine. The Iranians who were there were upper-class Western sympathizers; the rest of the crowd was European and American. Believe it or not, Iran was a swell place to go skiing, in part because very few Iranians could ski. It was never crowded, and conditions were excellent. Dry powder, packed underneath, soft on the surface. Up on top of the Alborz mountains with the white on white of the snow, sunny Persian skies with the few high clouds set off against the deep blue, you could forget the revolution for a few hours.

The Shah had the ski resort built as part of his modernization program. The Shah's relatives enjoyed skiing and the Shah was a real family man. All his relatives were millionaires in positions of power. While half the population was illiterate, and lived without electricity or running water, the Shah bought the most modern and expensive ski equipment to keep the upper class and the visiting foreigners happy. Military equipment like British-made Chieftain tanks and American jets were what seemed to make the Shah happy. In ten years Shah Reza Pahlavi had taken Iran from pawn to rook in the Persian Gulf. By 1978 Iran had become the strongest military power in the Middle East. Many people say the Shah's mistake was that he took power and wealth from the clerics. Others say he began to go nuts when he had himself crowned King in Persepolis in 1976. Persepolis was the famous city of hanging gardens renowned for its beauty. It was the city that Alexander the Great had, uncharacteristically, burned to the ground over two thousand years ago.

We skiied in a group all day and I never did get a chance to talk with Kelly. In fact I had the feeling she was avoiding me. The ski lifts stopped at four. As we drove back to Tehran we all talked about whether to stay or go. Americans, we had heard, were leaving the country in droves.

"I want to go," Janet said, staring at her arm. It was practically translucent. "But I had better ease off the heroin first."

"What about you guys?" I asked John and Carmel.

"I'm in no rush," John said. John was a very reticent guy. He had a beard that he would rub before he spoke. He was in Human Resources at Bell.

"I've heard the Ayatollah is coming back," Carmel said, jutting out her chin. "I'd like to stick around for that."

I wanted to hang around too; at least until the end of the school year in June, but I was worried. I hadn't gotten my last paycheck and I had this funny feeling the school wasn't going to re-open. Meanwhile my visa was in some government office, purportedly being renewed. Legally, I couldn't leave the country without an updated visa. If the school closed, I'd lose my work permit. Things were getting complicated and I was running out of money.

"What about you Kelly?" John asked.

"I'll stick until March—until I get my bonus."

"Are you two leaving together?" Carmel asked.

Kelly didn't say anything.

"I don't know, we haven't decided yet." I looked to Kelly for help. She was sitting in the passenger seat, but she continued staring straight ahead.

In January of 1979, the American Embassy proclaimed that Americans should keep a low profile and stick together. Kelly and I began spending most of our time during the day in a big house rented by Carmel, John and Janet. It was safer there than *Taj Rish*—the village where we rented our house. This house was located in one of the areas of Tehran still occupied by Americans and Western sympathizers. At night Kelly and I would drive surreptitiously home, making sure we got there before the nine o'clock curfew that had been imposed by the Shah.

One night early in January, John had a fire going in his fireplace. We were all settled into the Persian cushions on the Nain carpets John had bought the month before. The Nains are deep blue and off-white, made of silk and wool with knots so fine they are woven by young girls and boys whose small fingers can handle the intricate, tedious work. Nain carpets can only be bought in Iran and the buyer is not supposed to take them out of the country. These carpets, four feet by three feet, had cost John $3,000 apiece and they were a bargain. John was a vicious bargainer. He was tall and stood out with his red hair and beard. The rug merchants all called him the devil, but at the same time they seemed to get a kick out of him and he always ended up with great deals. They would quote a price and he would rub his beard and shake his head, insisting on his price until they relented.

So there we were, that January evening, leaning back on Persian cushions sitting on top of Nain carpets that were on top of a large, rough Turkoman rug. The cushions were stuffed woven horse blankets and saddle bags from the time when craftsmen and merchants from Russia, Iran and Afghanistan would gather in the summer outside Kabul, Afghanistan to trade their merchandise. John passed around a hash pipe while Carmel heated coals to smoke opium and Janet searched frantically for her stash of heroin. In Iran, heroin went for sixty bucks a gram and it was close to pure. At that time, Afghanistan was politically unstable, which made for an open road to the golden triangle of the Far East. Carmel and John were into the opium by the time Janet came downstairs with her smack. Opium and hash were very popular in Iran, or at least in Tehran. The taboo applied by the religious right to alcohol—drinking was not allowed—was not applied to drugs. Drugs were readily available and cheap. Opium, from which heroin is derived, is a hash-like high. It's a little heavier than hash, like the difference between swimming in a lake and swimming in the ocean.

"Heroin," John liked to say, "hits you like a tidal wave."

Kelly, a blue-eyed blonde whom no one would ever suspect of doing heroin, said to me that night: "You only live once. Let's give it a try."

So Kelly and I free-based heroin with Janet, running a lighter under a line of white powder placed on the aluminum wrapper from a Mr. Goodbar. I remember my head shooting up to the ceiling before floating down to settle back into the wall and then out and away from Iran to some sun-drenched lacuna of white sand and tropical fruit. I would have been happy to dream my life away in the South Pacific of my mind, but an hour or so later,

Kelly shook me out of my reverie. She said she wanted to go home. It was eight-thirty. A few minutes later Kelly and I tumbled into the car and we drove up Amirabad Avenue, past the Shah's Northern Palace with the guards in their jeeps in front of his gates. We waved to them and they returned our wave. We still considered them on our side.

At a few minutes before nine we parked at the bottom of the hill that led to our house. All we had to do was walk up one hundred stone steps to our gate and we were home, but we had underestimated the effects of the drug. My hands were trembling and I felt so weak I could hardly close the door of the car. When I did, it slammed shut like a gunshot in the stillness of the night. Kelly wasn't doing so well either. She leaned against the wall at the foot of the stairs, head hanging down to her knees. I put her arm over my shoulder and we began lunging up the stone slabs. Normally, I took those stairs at a run, but I was sapped of any strength. My teeth were chattering and my legs were stumps. Halfway up we stopped and Kelly threw up. By the time we reached the top, we were crawling.

Down the hill an army jeep pulled to a stop. The driver shined a flashlight on the stairs and from the roof behind us, a rifle fired. Kelly and I flattened ourselves on the ground outside our gate. The soldiers from the jeep exchanged shots with the revolutionary sniper who was firing from the roof of our neighbor's house. One soldier fired bursts from his Uzi. I reached up and opened the gate and we scrambled into the courtyard. We heard the jeep drive off, and we got up off the ground and ran into our house.

We spent the next morning in bed recuperating. That afternoon I walked down to the square to purchase some fresh bread. All the doors and the trunk of my car were open. The trunk was empty—tools and spare tire gone. Perplexed, I closed the car up and got in line. In Iran they have these little bakeries all over the city that make bread fresh every twenty minutes or so. People line up to wait for the hot bread. I exchanged greetings with Ali's father, my landlord, who was in line just in front of me. He asked me in Persian if I had hit a car recently on Shahanshahar Avenue.

"Who me?" I asked defensively.

He was a traditional Iranian, Ali's dad. His wife, who was standing beside him, had on a *chador* that, like a nun's habit, covered her from head to toe. All I could see was her eyes. They were not friendly.

"That's what the men told us when they broke into your car," she said in Persian.

All the other Iranians in the line were looking at me with distaste. I shrugged. I guessed it served me right. "Did you hear rifle shots last night?" I asked my landlord and his wife. "It sounded like they came from your roof." I stepped closer to Ali's dad: "Was it Ali?" I whispered.

My landlord frowned and looked away.

Later, when I told Kelly about it, she said, "You shouldn't have conned that guy you hit with your car."

"But it wasn't my fault," I said. "It was the soldiers who directed us onto that icy road."

"It's never your fault," she said. She was drying her hair. She had just stepped out of the shower. I stepped toward her to kiss her and she turned away. I pulled her toward me. "What's the matter?"

"I don't know," she said.

I kissed her and felt that connection that first brought us together. The feel of her skin and her smell beyond the citrus shampoo and beneath the soap. She came alive and responded then and we spent a couple of hours remembering that we knew each other in ways no one else did or ever would. She seemed to relax and I felt as if things would be okay.

Two weeks later John called us up and told us there was a big demonstration by the opposition in the works for that afternoon. Carmel would be covering it for the newspaper. I told John that Kelly and I would meet him at the entrance to the Northern Bazaar, just down the hill, at one o'clock.

That day in January in Tehran it was about seventy degrees, sunny, and everyone seemed to be in the streets. The Palace Guard was out in force in front of the Shah's summer residence—the huge palace he had retreated to was enclosed by towering walls and surrounded by elite troops who stood at attention or sat in jeeps with rifles in their arms. Soldiers lined the sidewalks.

Kelly and I could hear the mass of people before we rounded the corner that faced the bazaar at the bottom of the hill. More people than I'd ever seen: millions swarming in the streets. They carried flowers that they tossed at soldiers. They called out to the soldiers to throw down their guns and join them. The crazy part was that the demonstrators were all smiling and happy. They seemed to be enjoying themselves. I think that they were all surprised at how many people had turned out. I looked at the faces of the soldiers and I could see they were confused. They didn't seem to know what to make of the whole thing. It was then that I realized that it was over—the Shah wouldn't be in power much longer. There were too many people demonstrating and the soldiers seemed to have realized that the demonstrators, like them, were Iranians. It was just as Ali had said. Iranians couldn't kill other Iranians.

Kelly and I found John and Carmel and Janet at the entrance to the bazaar and it didn't take us long to see that we were the only Americans in sight. We thought if we could just get across the street we would go right up the hill and spend the afternoon at the house in *Taj Rish*. But as we started to cross the street a group of adolescents began dancing around us chanting, "Death to America." We turned and headed back toward the bazaar and by then the kids had alerted the crowd to our presence so I shouted to John, "We better run for it," and we took off into the bazaar. As the group started chasing us, I don't think it was related, some soldiers opened fire on the crowd. I saw half a dozen young men, students I think, shot down in the street. We flattened on the pavement until the shooting stopped, then we got up and ran.

We had to drag Janet along—she was in such bad shape. We wound our way in past the copperware, and the woolens, and the tapestries. When we got to the rug merchants, one of them waved us into his shop. We ducked in and he hid us in the back between the piles of rolled Persian carpets. John and I had both bought carpets from him. Janet was crying and John was trying to calm her down. Kelly had lost her confidence too. She was shaking. Only Carmel was her usual self.

"I wonder how bloody long this will take," she said.

We stayed in there for a couple of hours, long after the crowd had gone past chanting. Finally the rug merchant came in and told us we could go. He gave Janet, Carmel and Kelly chadors to wear and he snuck us out a side entrance that led to the street just south of the Shah's palace.

The crowd was still there, filling the streets, but now they were taunting the soldiers. They had infiltrated their ranks. I heard bursts of machine-gun fire, and I saw more demonstrators fall to the ground just up the hill. We scampered across the street and went through the woods back to the house Kelly and I rented. John, Janet and Carmel spent that night with us; none of us slept much. They returned to their house the next morning when the radio announced it was safe.

I went out for bread that morning. You wouldn't have known anything had happened. My neighbors greeted me warily. They were no longer angry about my accident but they no longer really trusted me either. When I got back to the house Kelly was packing. She had called Bell Helicopter. They had planes leaving for Athens, Greece every other day and she had decided to take one.

"What about your bonus?" I asked.

"Forget it," she said. "It won't do me much good if I'm not around to use it."

"But I thought you wanted to stay with me?"

She shook her head and closed her suitcase. "I don't ... I don't really feel as if I can depend on you anymore."

"What do you mean?" I opened a beer. "You're the one who doesn't sound like the same person."

"Why did we come here?" She zipped up her carry-on bag and stood it with her suitcase on the floor. "What were you thinking of?"

"What are you talking about? I didn't know there was going to be a revolution. You can't blame that on me."

"I don't," she said. "I just know I can't rely on you or anyone else. It just isn't working out." She started crying and I put my arms around her.

"Wait a minute," I said. I cupped my hands on her ass and pulled her closer.

"Knock it off," she said, pushing me away.

I could see that she was pissed at me. She didn't want me touching her. I suddenly wondered if I knew what she wanted. "Maybe we can straighten this out in Boston." I looked at her expectantly, hoping for something.

"I'm not going to Boston," she said. "I'm going home—to Buffalo."

I turned on the television. Apparently the Shah of Iran had also decided to leave. We watched him wave at crowds from his helicopter. He promised he would be back soon. Now I knew the school I worked at would not be reopening—the Shah and his wife had supported the school politically and financially, and without them, it would close for sure. Meanwhile the Ayatollah Khomeini was on his way to Iran from France, where the Shah's father had exiled him twenty years before.

"I want to leave too," I said to her, "but I don't work for Bell Helicopter."

"Take an Air Force evacuation plane," she said. "Pack your stuff and come with me, now."

I opened up another beer. She was right. I could take an Air Force plane. They were leaving daily. The problem was I needed to collect the check the school owed me and get my visa back from them. Plus, I had hoped to sell my car. I didn't want to leave.

John, Carmel and I saw Kelly off at the airport. The place looked like a refugee camp. There were people everywhere, entire families, from grandmothers to grandkids. Everyone seemed to be yelling or crying.

"I'll see you in Boston, or Buffalo, whatever," I said to Kelly, giving her a hug.

"Maybe," she said.

As we drove back to Tehran, John said that he and Janet were getting out that week too, before they closed the borders. Carmel announced that she was moving her stuff down to the Hilton. She had met an American reporter who told her that was where the action was.

That week I received notification in the mail that the school had officially closed, their funds were frozen—they wouldn't be able to pay me, and my visa had not been renewed. Now I was illegally in Iran and just about out of money.

Carmel and I put John and Janet on a Bell Helicopter evacuation plane that weekend and Carmel bought my car from me for a thousand bucks. I had paid five thousand for it eighteen months before. Carmel wasn't leaving until the Ayatollah Khomeini came. She wanted to see and hear him.

We watched the Ayatollah's parade—Carmel and I. It was a great day—millions of Iranians hopeful about the future. There weren't many Americans left in Iran but the Persians were in good spirits. I slept on the floor in Carmel's room at the Hilton that night. In the morning, early, I took a cab to the airport where I bribed an Iranian colonel with 250 American dollars and a box of cigars. "Please," I said. "I want you to have these." He didn't argue. He stamped my passport and told me never to return to Iran. The U.S. Air Force C-130 took me all the way to Athens for free. I sat in the wide belly dining on C-rations and thinking about Chieftain tanks, ski resorts and the echo of the song of the mullahs.

LUCKY CHARMS

I had hitched down to L.A. to visit my friend Paul back in the 70s when all you needed to get someplace was a thumb. I was going to school at U. of Montana in Missoula. I had a week off in the spring so I caught a lift to Seattle and then from there, three rides all the way down the coast. Paul was living in the valley, sharing a house with a guy named Spear. Spear's real name was Spheros, he was Greek, but everyone called him Spear. He was going to law school.

Spear was one of those guys whose dad bought him a new Corvette each year in high school. He was a couple of years older than Paul and me; a wiry guy with slick black hair and sharp cheekbones. His smile was a little scary; it was as if he was getting you comfortable but was ready to stab you with the knife he always carried if you said the wrong thing. We all thought Spear was really cool. Paul and I were actually friends with Spear's younger brother Chuckie, a much nicer guy, but when Paul found out that

Spear was living outside of L.A. and had plenty of room, he jumped at the opportunity and drove his Mustang out from Boston. We were all from Milton, a suburb south of Boston. Paul gave me a call at school telling me to come visit during spring break. I couldn't wait to get there.

It wasn't till I got to the house (my last ride was nice enough to drop me there) that I found out that Spear had brought this hooker out from Boston with him. I had heard that Spear used to hang out in a strip joint called the Two O'Clock in the Combat Zone in Boston. I don't know what the girl's real name was; she went by Star. She was nineteen, attractive although not exactly pretty. Her face was too angular and her hair was a brassy bottle blond. She had a tattoo of a snake running around one of her arms and back then, nice girls didn't sport tattoos. The first time I met her, she was leaning against the kitchen counter drinking coffee in white high heels, tight jeans, a tee shirt and no bra. Spear had told her to move out of her bedroom and onto the couch so I could stay in her room. I told him I was fine on the couch but he insisted so she resented me right off.

"Unless you want her in there," Spear said to me with that edgy smile of his.

"No, that's okay," I said.

"Just don't fuck with my shit," she said, glaring at me.

The next morning when I got up, Paul was sitting in the kitchen, eating some cereal. "Help yourself man," he said.

"Lucky Charms?"

"There's other stuff up there." He motioned with his head.

I opened one of the cabinets and pulled down a box of Frosted Flakes.

"Ah, those are Star's," Paul said. "Take a look in that cabinet."

I looked back. It was like a little corner store with sugar, coffee, salt and pepper, cereal, peanuts, bread, a kind of survival kit.

"She keeps all her own food in there. In fact, she had a lock on it for a couple of weeks until I convinced her I wasn't going to take any of it."

I put the tiger back and poured myself some Lucky Charms. When I put milk on them, the milk turned green and blue from the dyed chunks of marshmallow.

Paul had to go to work. He drove a delivery truck for a construction company. I was putting my bowl in the sink when Spear came out of his room.

"Find something to eat?" he asked me.

I nodded. "How's the Corvette running?" I asked.

"Spends more time in the shop than out of it," he said. He looked over at Star who was still asleep on the couch. "Do you want a blow job?" he said to me. He wasn't smiling. It appeared to be a straightforward question.

I hesitated. I wanted to say no but I didn't want to appear ungrateful.

"Not from me," he said, smiling, "from her."

"No, I'm good," I said.

Star sat up. "Your friend thinks he's too good for me." She stretched and yawned. Her nipples were sticking out. She caught me looking.

"They do that in the morning," she said and laughed.

Now I was getting hard and with my gym shorts on, it was obvious.

"You may not want me but your dick seems to." She laughed again and looked at Spear. "Who does he look like?"

"I don't know, who?" Spear rubbed his neck.

"The cowboy in *Rawhide,*" she said.

"You're right, he looks like Rowdy Yates. I'm taking a shower," Spear said, going into the bathroom.

Star took her top off and cupped her breasts. I took a couple of awkward steps towards her.

"No way are you getting any of this Rowdy," she said. She walked across the room in her panties and into the bathroom with Spear.

I went back into Star's room, closed the door and flopped on the bed. I needed a couple of hours more of sleep. I hadn't slept hardly at all getting there and now I was wondering if I'd made a mistake taking Paul up on his invitation. I didn't know what to make of Star and I couldn't figure out why Spear would want her there. Nonetheless, I fell asleep envisioning sex with Star. We'd start out standing up and move to various pieces of furniture: the bureau, the chair, the couch. I imagined she knew a few techniques I had never even heard of. I had to roll onto my back to get to sleep.

When I woke up it was noon. The house was empty. I guessed that Spear had left for class. His car was not in the driveway. I walked down the street and found a little Mexican restaurant where I had a veggie burrito and a Corona. Three Coronas later I meandered back to the house, a little unsteady. I found a lounge chair in the yard and dozed in the sun. The rumbling sound of Paul's Mustang GT shook me awake.

He had picked up some steaks. He threw them on the grill and we were just finishing them up when Spear pulled into the driveway.

"Where's Star?" I asked when he got out.

"You like Star?" he asked, narrowing his eyes.

"No, I was just curious."

"Hey," Spear said, "she's yours for the taking amigo. I wish I'd never brought her out here, believe me. I thought she was going to make me some money but it turns out that she doesn't even like to turn tricks. She wants to get out of the life." Spear laughed. "Why don't you take her back to school with you when you leave?"

Paul seemed to be getting a big kick out of this. "She's at this bar down the street, the Roadhouse," he said. She's a waitress there."

"She's trying to get on as a stripper," Spear said. "We'll go there. Maybe she can give you a lap dance."

"She's pretty good," Paul said. "She's been practicing on me."

"She sucks." Spear spit on the ground, pulled out a pack of Camels and fired one up.

A couple of hours later Spear left in his car. I asked Paul if he wanted a beer for the road.

"Have to be careful drinking and driving around here," Paul said. "I've been arrested twice for D.U.I. Second time I had to pay a thousand bucks and take a class. Next time they yank my license."

"Just one before we go," I said, tossing him a Bud tall boy.

The bar was a huge sprawling three-story surrounded by parking lots. We found a spot for the pony in back. Paul pointed out Spear's red Corvette parked between a string of pick-ups.

The place was packed. I was surprised to see a lot of women. Paul told me the strippers worked the top floor. We climbed the stairs and found Spear at a table. He had shots of tequila, a salt shaker and lime wedges and a couple of bottles of Bud waiting for us.

I wanted to ask where Star was but I didn't want Spear to get on my case so I kept my mouth shut and downed the tequila. I was chasing it with the Bud while watching a cute blond take off her police officer outfit.

"I'll bet you the next round you can't choke me," Spear said to me.

I did not know what to say.

"He locks his throat," Paul said. "Try it. You can't hurt him."

I was going to get the next round anyway so I put my beer down while Spear turned his chair so I could stand in front of him. "Tell me to stop if it hurts," I said.

He gave me the finger. I proceeded to put my hands, clawlike, around his throat and choke him. I squeezed as hard as I could. A crowd began to gather around. They egged me on. I wasn't getting anywhere and my hands were beginning to cramp. I wondered if I could get arrested for assault. Spear would sue me. I'd be in debt to him for the rest of my life. I let go. There was a moan from the crowd. The choking seemed to have no effect whatsoever on Spear. "Jose Gold," he said.

In a couple of hours Paul was pretty wasted. I had stopped drinking after the third round. Spear had said he wanted to take a look around and he disappeared into the crowd. At some point Star appeared. She seemed to be dressed up as a French maid. She looked pretty sexy. She pushed me into an empty chair near the bar, sat on my lap and blew in my ear. I was not entirely immune to her charms.

"Do you want a lap dance?" she said to me.

I thought about how much money I had. "Not tonight," I said.

She stood up. "Back to the grind," she said.

Paul and I decided to leave. On the way out, we bumped into Spear holding hands with a tall, thin beauty with long blond hair. She wavered on her heels. He held his car keys up in front of him. "Let me take your Mustang," he said to Paul. "I might need the back seat."

Paul took the keys to the Corvette and gave Spear the keys to the Mustang.

"So we get to drive the Corvette, cool," I said as we searched the parking lot. "Was that chick drunk, or what?"

"He picks them up and gives them Dilaudids," Paul said.

"What are Dilaudids?"

"They're downs, really strong. The girls love them," Paul laughed.

I noticed he was swaying. "Lemme drive," I said.

"I'm all right," Paul said, smiling.

We were pulled over just as we drove out of the parking lot. The cop had us both get out of the car. He shined a flashlight on our licenses and had us walk, count backwards and touch our nose with one finger.

"You drive," he said to me. I couldn't believe our luck.

About a mile down the road, Paul asked me to pull over. He got out and threw up.

When he got back in he said: "I can't believe he let us go. I've got to get out of this state. If he had looked me up, he definitely would have taken me in. They'd be booking me right now."

The road was empty. I took it up to sixty in first gear. The big engine roared with power and the wide tires gripped the road, but in second gear, going ninety through an S turn, the car turned sideways and skidded off the road to the edge of a cliff overlooking a canyon.

We got out and stared over the edge.

"Fuckin A," Paul said and laughed.

I reached in, put it in neutral, and backed the car up to the shoulder.

"You all right to drive?" Paul asked.

"Yeah, it was just a little more power than I expected."

The Mustang was in the driveway. I pulled in beside it. I grabbed a couple of Coronas from the fridge as Paul turned on the TV. He found a classic games channel that was playing the Celtics/L.A. game where Wilt scored a hundred points. He lit a joint and passed it to me. I was just falling into a nod when the door to Spear's room opened and Spear walked out in his boxers, propping up the beautiful blond. She looked like a scarecrow without any clothes on. He pulled her into the living room and when he let go of her arm, she slumped to the floor on her hands and knees. Her beautiful hair cascaded over her head.

"You guys want to do her?" Spear asked.

Paul looked at me. This was not my idea of cool. "Not me. You go ahead," I said.

"My room's a mess," Paul said to Spear.

"Use Star's room," Spear said.

Paul lifted the girl to her feet. "What's her name?" he said to Spear.

Spear ran his fingers through his hair. "Shit," he said. "Can't remember, Jenine, something like that."

Paul took the girl into Star's room. I couldn't believe it. What was he thinking? Was having sex with that girl even legal? Spear sat down on the couch and we watched the game.

"So," Spear said to me, "how's it goin?"

"It's goin all right," I said, although actually I wasn't feeling too comfy. In fact, I was beginning to think I should get the hell out the next day before something went seriously awry. Spear was not as cool as I thought he was. He was sort of a psycho.

We heard a truck pull into the driveway.

"Shit," Spear said, "That's Star. She gets a ride from one of the other girls."

Star came in through the kitchen door. She stood beside us, staring at the TV. We heard a series of thumps emanating from her room. We all turned and looked at the door.

Star walked around the couch in front of Spear. "Who the fuck is in my room?" she said.

"Shut up and grab a beer," Spear said.

"Look, you bring girls home, okay. I get that. I don't exactly expect you to marry me."

Spear scoffed and stood up. "You want another?" he said to me.

Star pushed him back down onto the couch.

"That's my fucking room!" she said. "First you give it to this asshole and now Paul is banging some skank in there."

Spear looked at me with his eyebrows up. He found this pretty funny and I could see he was about to laugh. Then he did laugh.

"Fuck you," Star said. She marched over to her room and opened the door. "Get out!" she yelled.

We heard a drawer open and shut.

"Oh no," Spear said.

When she emerged from her room, she was holding a gun, a .38. Her hands were shaking.

I ducked and Spear stood up.

"Baby," Spear said. He had his hands in front of him.

I peeked over the top of the couch. Then I realized that a couch would not do much to protect me and I sat up. She turned the gun toward me.

"Sweety," Spear said, taking a step toward her.

An ad came on with a couple of blonds selling Budweiser. She pointed the gun at the television and shot it. She'd put a hole right in the middle of the screen; the television kept going for a few seconds and then died.

"Nice shot," Paul said. Paul stood behind Star in the doorway to her room with a sheet draped around him. He looked like a guest at a toga party. Meanwhile Jenine, nude, had staggered out to the kitchen sink. She seemed to be after some water.

Star dropped the gun to her side and began sobbing. Spear gave her a hug. "It's okay, doll," he said, relieving her of the gun. He turned and winked at me.

I was shaking but at the same time I felt sorry for Star and for the girl at the sink and I didn't like being winked at by Spear who apparently thought I shared his point of view.

I was suddenly exhausted and I lay back on the couch and fell asleep. About an hour later I woke up. It was quiet and the lights had been turned out. Everyone had gone to bed apparently. I wondered if Star would mind if I crashed with her. I didn't want to get her angry, but the couch was pretty uncomfortable and I thought she might even appreciate a little company.

Her door was unlocked. She was lying face down under a single sheet. I pulled my shirt off and dropped my jeans and climbed in beside her. She opened one eye. "You've got a lot of balls," she said.

I ran my hand down her spine.

"Turn over on your back," she said.

There was just enough light to see the outline of her head. I heard her tear something plastic and then felt her mouth slip a ring over my dick. I felt the sleeve and the pressure of her mouth. I was already hard.

"Can I put it in?" I asked.

She rolled over and I climbed on and entered her. It didn't take me long to come.

"You can give me the money in the morning," she said.

"What?" I said, "give me a break."

"Spear will know. He'll make me get the money from you. If it were up to me, believe me, I wouldn't charge you."

"How'd you get into this business?" I propped myself up on one elbow and looked at her. She looked a lot younger in the dim light. It was as if she had removed that hard shell she always wore.

"A friend of mine was doing it and making money."

"Paul told me you're from South Boston."

"D Street projects." She turned away from me. "At least Spear got me out of there."

I thought about that for a minute. "What do you want to do?"

She snorted. "I don't know what Spear was thinking but I told him I didn't want to turn tricks for him when I came out here. I thought maybe I could go to hairdressing school. There's one not too far from here. I've already applied. Hey, I'm just trying to follow the American dream and be happy just like everyone else."

The American dream? Happy? Was she serious? I wanted to ask her but she had turned on her side and seemed to want to go to sleep.

When I woke up I could hear Star and Spear arguing but I couldn't make out what they were saying. I got up, pulled on my jeans and walked into the kitchen where Spear was drinking coffee.

I poured myself a cup.

"Help yourself," Spear said, but he didn't sound friendly. "You owe Star a hundred bucks," he said. "That's her rate."

I just nodded. I pulled out my wallet and looked inside. I had exactly 108 dollars. I took out four twenties and two tens and handed them to Star.

"Thanks," she said. She gave me a look that was supposed to mean something but I wasn't sure what. She gave half the money to Spear.

He put the fifty bucks in his top pocket. "No freebies unless I say so," he said. He looked at his Rolex. "If you want a ride," he said to Star, "we better get a move on."

For a second I wondered where Star was going but I shook it off. I didn't want to care about her, and I'd had just about enough of Spear. She went into her room to change. I drank my coffee on the couch while staring at the hole in the television screen. I suddenly wished I had brought a camera with me. It would have made a cool picture. When Star came out she handed me my shirt.

Paul got up just after they left. I asked him if he'd drop me at the entrance to the highway. It was about twenty minutes away.

"Heading back early?" He was looking in the cabinets.

"I'm out of money," I said.

"I can lend you a few bucks," he said.

I asked Paul what happened to the thin blond.

"Spear called her a cab. Shit," he said, "I'm out of Lucky Charms."

An hour later, Paul pulled his car over just after the on-ramp to the highway. "Let me give you some money," he said, reaching for his wallet.

"I'm all right," I said.

"I've got to get out of here too," he said. "Maybe I'll see you back in Milton this summer."

I got out and stretched. I watched Paul drive off. It was already hot and hazy and it was only 11:00. With luck I'd be out of California by dawn. It would be cooler up north. I was anxious to get back to school, back onto the solid ground of the plains where things made a little more sense. It was a little too edgy in California. In a couple of months, Spear would be getting out of law school and opening his own practice. The thought of it just made me shudder. That's when I noticed the folded up bill in my shirt pocket. Star must have put it in my pocket before she handed the shirt to me. I took the bill out and turned it over—Ben Franklin stared back at me. He was not happy.

LUCK

Nick thought he'd finally found a space for his Audi. He had to be careful where he parked. It was less than a year old and was already scarred with nicks and scratches (welcome to Boston). He'd wedged it into a tight space between two SUVs before he noticed the no parking sign. When he got out of the car, he stood back and looked the car over. It was filthy with winter road grit. He'd have to take it to the car wash. It was a great car, although if he had a few more bucks to spend he would have gone for the A6. His wife had really been the one who paid for it. She was the lawyer. He was a teacher; he made less than half what his wife brought home. *Damn*, he said to himself, *it is really cold.* He hated February. He checked his watch, ten past four; as usual he was late. He had stopped at Brookline Liquor Mart for beer and wine. As he walked up the hill to the adoption center he slipped on the ice and fell.

"God damn it!" he said. He managed to catch himself with one hand but then he banged his elbow. He got up and tried to brush the sand off his topcoat. He had bought it at Barney's mid-winter sale. It was a good deal but it still cost a fortune. *Money*, he shook his head.

He should have been used to it by now. That's the way it was in this damn country. He caught his reflection in the glass door. He'd have to have his coat cleaned. Plus, he needed a haircut. He shook his head. He was always shaking his head.

It was warm inside the building. His wife, early as always, was waiting for him. Nick gave her a quick kiss. She looked good, if a little tired. She had her black suit on. The skirt was short and her heels made her look tall. He liked the new hair-do. She had to get up early every morning to blow it dry so it would be straight. She had recently applied lipstick and make-up.

A secretary told them they could go into the counselor's office. Nick took a deep breath. Soon he and his wife would be able to focus on the child they were going to adopt. They were upsizing their family, restructuring their life in a good way, finally. He wanted the child. The child would change everything. Isn't that what everyone said?

The process, though, was like applying to college. They had passed the home study. The counselor had visited their house and approved of it. She had interviewed them separately and together. They had filled out forms, written about their values ("Family is very important") and gotten friends to write recommendations ("The Browns will make great parents"). It should have been a walk in the park. Weren't they both professionals? Well, teachers were sort of like professionals except that no one respected them and they didn't make any money.

They had signed up for an infant from Guatemala. It was going to cost twenty thousand dollars. They had a photo of a baby girl who was one month old. She had brown eyes and a little brown fuzz on her head. She appeared to be smiling. If everything went smoothly, they would have her in a couple of months. He was just beginning to allow himself to get excited about the idea of having a new little person in their house—their home. He and his wife agreed they would share in the parental duties. He was going to be a good father. No screw-ups. Just take it slow and work at it. He sighed and felt the pressure go out with his breath.

They were meeting today because the counselor had been waiting for a "CORI"—a criminal activity report on him from the FBI. He was a little nervous because he didn't know whether he had an official arrest record or not. He had written on the form that he had never been arrested or convicted of a crime but he had in fact been arrested. Twenty-five years before, when he was twenty-one, a senior in college, but the case had been dismissed and his lawyer had told him there would be no record of it.

Twenty-five years ago. Senior year at UMass, Zoo-Mass, they called it. He was living with Albie, Gillis, and Goody at a student ghetto called Swiss Village. They had a party. The parties at UMass had been wild. All their college friends were there and friends of friends too. He and Gillis had gone out to get some booze and at the liquor store had picked up these two cute local girls. When they returned to the party, the crowd went through the booze fast and the two local girls circulated to collect more money for beer and vodka. The girls were climbing all over the college guys, rubbing up against them, grabbing them between their legs. Sometimes the girls would kiss each other and fondle each other's breasts. Soon the girls had a wad of cash and Nick drove them back to the liquor store where they stocked up with cases of beer and fifths of vodka, tequila, bourbon. They put the booze in the back seat and all three of them squeezed in the front seat of Nick's Challenger. Nick had started driving back when one of the girls unzipped his pants, pulled him out and gave him head. He came at a red light, horns blaring behind him, the girls giggling.

When they got back to the party the girls made drinks for everyone, handed out beer. A lot of people had taken Percocets. Joints were going around. Albee had the speakers from his bedroom in the living room and the stereo was blasting the Rolling Stones. Everyone was wasted. Girls from upstairs had come down and were dancing on the coffee table until it cracked in half and then they got up on the kitchen counter. About then the two local girls initiated an orgy. People started having sex all over the place—on the couch, in chairs, on the floor. One of the college girls lost consciousness and had to be brought to the infirmary. Someone put his foot through one of the speakers and Albee just pulled out a back-up speaker and hooked it up.

There had been a lot of parties at UMass, lots of drugs. God, senior week a couple of Albee's friends returned from a trip to Columbia with a pound of cocaine and put the bag on the new coffee table in the living room and said, "Help yourself guys." Really, senior year was kind of a blur. Maybe that wasn't one party he remembered but a few parties blended together like a mixed drink in his mind. Now Albee was a lawyer and a slumlord. Gillis was out in California, in and out of jail for assault, breaking and entering, stealing cars. Gillis had done too much acid in college. He could have been a poster boy for the ad: this is your brain on drugs.

Anyway, Nick had stumbled out of the party to pee when the Amherst police pulled up. One cop went into the party and broke it up and the other grabbled Nick and put him into the back seat of the police car. They were arresting him for being drunk and disturbing the peace. Was he drunk? Yeah, but so were Albie, Gillis, Goody and everybody else at the party. Nick was the one taken into custody because he was peeing outside when the cops drove up. It was just bad luck.

This was just after the administration had changed their policy at UMass. When he was a freshman, the college had protected the students. They didn't want the bad publicity of arrests, but that was before the nationwide strike against Vietnam when the colleges were closed down for a month in May of 1970. After that, the Amherst police were called in if there was a problem—drinking, drugs, disturbing the peace.

The Amherst police were housed in an old brick building. Inside, the arresting officer removed the cuffs and Nick was told to empty his pockets onto the counter in front of the sergeant's desk. It was when he reached for his wallet that he remembered he had a joint in it. He always kept a joint in his wallet not so much because he liked marijuana but because girls liked marijuana. He thought he could get the joint out and hide it or maybe eat it or throw it away. He dropped his wallet on the floor but when he reached down for it, the sergeant reacted. "He's trying something!" he yelled and leaped over his desk and tackled Nick. Nick and the sergeant wrestled on the floor and tumbled back into the wall. There was a painting of a fisherman in a rowboat on the wall and the painting fell off the wall on top of them.

"He's wrecking the painting!" the sergeant called out and two more officers appeared and jumped in and pulled Nick to his feet. Nick remembered feeling as if he had entered the wonderful world of pro wrestling and he laughed.

"You think this is funny?" the sergeant said. The sergeant grabbed Nick by his collar and held him against the wall. One of the cops picked up Nick's wallet and discovered the joint on the floor. "Look at this," he said.

"Well, we've got you now," the sergeant said. "Book this bastard for possession." He cackled and shook his head.

One of the cops pushed Nick down the corridor and put him into a cell and locked the door.

"The damn kid ruined the painting," he heard the sergeant say.

That was a Friday night. On Monday morning he was arraigned. He'd called Albee to get a local lawyer for him. In the courtroom, the judge announced the case, his lawyer and the D.A. approached the bench and whispered something to the judge, and the judge hit the bench with his gavel and said, "Case dismissed."

That's what Nick thought he said but really, he couldn't remember. Maybe he said, case continued. His lawyer told him not to worry about it. It was over.

The adoption counselor closed the door and told them to take a seat.

"I'm afraid I have bad news for you," she said. She was quite pleasant looking, the counselor. She had a comforting smile. She was wearing gray slacks and a white mohair sweater. Her short hair looked like it had recently been washed. "The criminal activity report, Mr. Brown, is not good. It isn't so much the drunkenness and disturbing the peace. They don't care about that. It's the 'possession of a controlled substance.' I know it seems silly but anything with drugs and they won't approve the adoption."

"Who? Who won't approve the adoption?" His wife looked suddenly stricken, as if she had been hit in the chest. The color drained out of her face.

"The government of Guatemala," the counselor said. "I know this is hard," the counselor went on quickly, "but other countries are not as strict about this kind of thing."

They were sitting in chairs that were side by side and he reached over to take his wife's hand but she drew it away from him onto her lap. She was crying. The counselor got up from behind her desk, came around and took one of her hands. "I'm sorry," she said. She glanced at him. "This must be difficult for you too, Mr. Brown."

Nick looked up at the adoption counselor. He realized he had to say something. "I'm sorry I didn't say anything earlier," he said, "but when it happened, my lawyer told me there wouldn't be any arrest record."

The counselor handed him a photocopy of the report. "It says right on it that the charges were dismissed after a continuance without a finding," she said, "but there's still a record of it and so, I'm sorry to say, we can't go ahead with the adoption. I suggest you go home, take some time to think about it and then maybe try another country."

So they had been rejected. He had been rejected by the government of Guatemala as an unfit parent. Nick and his wife stood outside in front of the adoption agency on the sidewalk. There was a parking ticket in his window and he cursed. On top of everything else, he gets a ticket.

"I know how you feel," his wife said and stepped toward him and put her arms around his waist. He didn't tell her it was the ticket he was cursing about, not the adoption.

She was way too good for him; that was for sure. She should have married another lawyer instead of a fuck-up like him. She and the lawyer could have adopted kids together and had a family. They would have a nanny to help. He felt her leg between his legs and he started to get aroused and felt embarrassed and stepped away from her. God, he was an asshole.

"We'll talk later," she said. She was still crying. She turned and walked toward her car. It was a Volvo wagon, a much more sensible choice than his. She looked good, his wife, but she was getting older. They were both getting old. They were in their forties. He was forty-six, already too old for the adoption rules for a lot of countries.

He took the ticket off the windshield and got into his car: twenty-five dollars for the privilege of parking illegally in Brookline to find out they were not getting a new member of the family. It was his fault. It was all his fault, right? Or was it a stupid rule, this rule about a drug arrest—one fucking joint, disturbing the peace, twenty-five years ago? He should have been a lawyer. If he had been a lawyer maybe he could have "disappeared" his record. The United States was a petty country to arrest people for marijuana. It was a stupid country not to value schools. He worked hard. His wife worked harder. He needed to lighten up a little. He took his wallet out. In it, he still kept a joint. He had some matches in the glove compartment. The minute he took a hit, he felt better. He pulled a Harpoon Ale out of the bag on the floor and opened it up. "That's the ticket," he said. He put the joint in the ashtray and pulled out onto the street and turned on the radio. Some guy was talking about how optimists were more successful and well-adjusted. Maybe that was his problem. He wasn't optimistic. He was picturing the little girl's face as he went through a light just as it was turning red. He and his wife had come up with a list of names: Lucia, Maria, Rosa, Isabella. Now, it was as if they had lost a child or maybe she had lost them. He shook his head. He saw a cruiser pull up behind him with the flashers going. He hit the brakes and pulled over, spilling the beer onto his coat. He put the half empty beer back into the carton and hit the button to open the window.

"Could I see your license and registration, sir?" The cop stood looking down at him.

As Nick handed his information to him, the cop sniffed. Then he noticed the open beer. "Step out of the car, sir," he said. He put one hand over his gun while he reached for his handcuffs.

"Come on," Nick said, laughing. "What are you going to do? Arrest me?"

A RARE NIGHT OUT

I was happy. I had just finished taking a class called "The Politics of English Composition." It sounds dull, I know, but I teach English Composition so I found it interesting. My wife and I were sitting in a new Vietnamese restaurant that had opened in Harvard Square. Our six-year-old daughter was spending the night at my sister's—it was a rare night out during the week. My wife and I have always enjoyed sampling small restaurants and new food. My wife had ordered Vietnamese vermicelli with lemongrass and I took a chance on shrimp and green beans with ginger and garlic. I was still excited about the class and I was explaining a theory. "According to Ann Berthoff, language builds the human world," I said. "And this other guy, Burke, claims that we create reality out of language."

My wife, Gretta, was looking at me funny. She seemed to be pretty tired. She'd been up early that morning working on a project. She's an architect. She got this sarcastic look—eyebrows up, mouth turned down at the corners—and she said, "That's really interesting, Robert."

I asked her if I could try a little vermicelli and she said sure. The vermicelli was so light it seemed to disappear on my tongue and what remained was the taste of lemongrass and a spicy red curry. It was better than what I had ordered. I have to admit that her sarcasm threw me a little because I *did* think what I had said was interesting. I had always been interested in theory, but I had been feeling a little out of touch teaching at a community college—that's why I had taken the course. On an impulse, I thought I would try something we had been talking about in class—problematizing. "What do you mean by the word *interesting?*" I asked.

Gretta put her fork down. I could see she was really tired—she had that pale, haggard look. My wife is quite attractive. In fact, she has grown more attractive with age. She has emerald green eyes and porcelain skin that form a nice contrast to her red hair. When she was young she wore her hair long, but now it is blown straight with a dryer and blunt cut at her neck with bangs that fall straight across just above her eyes, and the effect is striking. Of course, when she's worn out, it's a different story. The porcelain begins to crack and the emeralds to lose their luster. "Well," she said, "something interesting would be something that makes you perk up and listen." She was leaning forward with both elbows on the table. She held a fork full of vermicelli in the air. The vermicelli slipped off her fork onto her lap.

"Something that makes you listen?" I asked, "Something that acts on you? You don't have anything to do with it?"

She was nodding. "OK," she said, "you have something to do with it." She dipped her napkin in her water glass and rubbed at her skirt, scowling.

"What do you have to do with it being interesting?" I asked, spooning more of my shrimp onto my plate. "What I mean is," I went on, "is talking about what's interesting interesting?"

"Yes," she said. "Dammit, I can't get this out. Yes, okay? It does."

I could see she was angry about her skirt but I pressed on. I couldn't help it. "What makes it interesting?"

"Thinking about it," she said.

I smiled. It had worked. "Exactly," I said.

She threw her napkin in my face. "Asshole," she said.

When I took the napkin off my face I could see she was furious.

"Sometimes you can be so damn belligerent," she said. "What am I? One of your students?"

"No," I said. "I'm trying to be the opposite of belligerent—problematizing offers *you* the opportunity to define the discussion—to change it and by changing it—to change your view and mine."

"Really," she said, stabbing her fork into her food. "So you weren't manipulating me into saying what I said?"

"No," I said, "not at all. I was interested in your point of view." Of course she was absolutely right. I had manipulated her.

"Is this what I'm going to have to listen to for the next twenty years?" She signaled for the check.

I took a couple of quick mouthfuls and then told her I'd go get the car and pick her up out front. The car was a couple of blocks away. We had taken her car—the Volvo wagon. I got in and started it up. I turned on the heater and the seat warmer. I suddenly wondered, if I took off right now, how long would it take me to drive to Mexico? It had taken about three days to hitch there when I was twenty years old. I wouldn't want to take her car though. I'd want to stop at home and take my car—the Audi. I pulled out and drove towards the restaurant just as she stepped into the street. The Volvo had a turbo. If I gunned it, I could pin her between her car and the one parked just behind her. It would almost certainly kill her. I looked around. The street was empty. Just then another couple came out of the restaurant. I realized I'd been holding my breath and I let it out. I pulled the car up beside her, reached across the front seat and opened the passenger door. My wife climbed in.

On the drive home I told her she was almost out of gas and asked if she wanted to stop for some.

"I'll get it tomorrow," she said. She asked if I had made a dentist appointment for Kate.

I told her I hadn't but would the next day.

The house seemed quiet without Kate. It felt terribly empty. I poured us a cognac and we sat on opposite sides of the couch. We had decided for a number of reasons to have only one child. We believed in population control. We were worried about the future. We were concerned we wouldn't be able to devote the time necessary because of our careers. Our careers were important to us and in addition we wanted to travel and where we could do that quite easily with one child, two would make things difficult. Still, there were times when I wondered if we wouldn't have been better off with two or even three children. I told Gretta I was sorry for having started the discussion about the word "interesting."

Gretta said she was afraid we were developing separate lives—that soon we wouldn't have anything in common.

"Don't be ridiculous," I said, and then I realized I had become angry. I didn't really enjoy having a napkin thrown in my face at a restaurant. It was humiliating, almost like being slapped. The only time that ever happened to me was at a ninth grade dance when I had put my hand on Karen Lipsky's breast. In addition, Gretta had ridiculed the subject I'd become interested in and virtually said that she didn't care about it and didn't want to hear about it. And somewhere beneath the surface I had this gnawing feeling she had manipulated me into deciding not to have more children. She made it seem like it was our decision but I was the one who got the vasectomy. I wondered if I could have it reversed. Then we could get divorced and I could remarry and have a big family—five, maybe six children. Kate could come to visit us in the summer. Gretta would drop her off at the end of the long path leading to the ranch I would live on with this new family of mine. There would be horses. We could all go riding together—the whole family but not Gretta because she hated horses.

Gretta was right—a chasm had opened up between us. I felt as if I was talking to a complete stranger. I could sense she felt the same way. How had we met anyway? A mutual acquaintance had introduced us at an art opening of his. I had to admit I had never understood the appeal of his art. He did all these paintings of shovels. I hadn't talked to Michael for years but Gretta would occasionally meet him for lunch. I suddenly wondered if there was anything going on between them.

"I have to go to bed," she finally said, taking my hand. "Are you coming?"

When we made love, I couldn't stop thinking of everything we had been talking about and I was still angry with her. I probably should have been impotent, but I wasn't. Instead I was going on automatic. Being a male I guess. Representing my gender.

Long after she had fallen asleep, I lay awake. I was thinking about what a leap of faith marriage is. It was really interesting when you thought about it. Really interesting. I looked over at my wife. I loved her but I didn't really like her at all at the moment. I knew she didn't like me either. I imagined the feeling would pass. I got up out of bed and poured myself another cognac. I took a melatonin and sat in the living room looking at *Car and Driver.* I was waiting for that nice numb feeling. The Audi was almost four years old. I was ready for something new.

KICK-BOXING WITH INGRID

From the first day of class I had been obsessed with her. We were conferencing one on one in the cafeteria. I had told her she was going to get an "A" as long as she kept up the good work. We were wrapping it up when I blurted out, "You know, we could meet sometime for coffee, off-campus, if you like." I sneezed. I had a brutal cold.

I immediately regretted saying it. I was twice her age, married with two teenage boys. It was absurd—the notion that she would be in any way interested in me.

"Ya, that would be nice," she said.

I nodded. Meeting her out of class was risky, not just to my marriage, but to my job. I would be violating the sexual harassment clause in my contract. I was no tenured professor. I was an adjunct hired on one-year renewable contracts.

Ingrid was, however, a knock-out—high cheekbones, full lips, eyes the color of the sky in June. And I just knew, from the way she stared at me in class, the way she leaned forward in her seat and hung on every witty, insightful word I uttered, that I had a shot with her. I figured that, for once, it just might be worth it. I had never taken such a risk in the ten years I'd been teaching and the fifteen years I'd been married.

That night Ingrid emailed me that she'd be happy to have coffee sometime (my email address was on the syllabus; this was ten years ago, before everyone started texting).

I emailed her back asking if she'd like to meet the next morning. She said she didn't have any classes. Well, neither did I. We agreed to meet at Jake's, a couple of miles away from the campus and not far from where I lived. Jake's is one of those homey places full of high-fat baked goods and specialty coffees. I stopped there once a week or so. The woman who got our coffee called me sweetheart. She called everyone honey or sweetheart. She was always smiling, but that day she looked at me with raised eyebrows. Ingrid had a caffè latte with unsweetened licorice.

"I don't like sweets," she said.

I thought this tied in with her sophistication—another justification for my coming onto her. I asked her to tell me about where she had grown up.

"It was a small town," she said, "near Oslo. My father was an engineer. I have two older brothers."

Her father would probably be about my age. Her brothers would be much younger. I pictured meeting their puzzled looks. They wouldn't know what to think of me. They would be tall with blond hair and would be wearing red-checked, flannel shirts. I would help them chop wood as the father looked on. The older brother would make a joke about chopping off my head. They would all laugh heartily. "What do you *vant* with our Ingrid?" one of the brothers would ask me. They would exchange edgy glances.

"I want to marry her," I'd say. "I love her."

"Ingrid tells me you are married with two sons," the father would say.

"Yes," I'd say, "but I'm getting a divorce."

In fact, I did not want a divorce. I loved my wife. My wife was smart, successful, attractive, a great mother and friend. I really had no complaints about her. I'd been faithful for the fifteen years we'd been married. Plus I loved my two sons. The older one, at fourteen, could be a pain—a real whiner. The younger one, the thirteen-year-old, was way too charming for his own good, but I would never want to leave them. Really, I've never understood how people get divorced. These people who have two or three families with different sets of children—it's totally beyond me. I remember breaking up with girlfriends, before I was married; it would send me to the edge of an emotional cliff with a voice in my head saying, jump, jump. I'd be a wreck for months.

Ingrid sipped her coffee and asked me whether I had plans with my family for spring vacation. I must have mentioned that I was married in class.

"No," I said, blowing my nose. "How about you?" I was evading her question. I didn't want to go into my family life with her. Instead I wanted to stare at her mouth. Her lips were rich and thick. One side of her mouth curved down a little. I wanted to kiss her—one of those kisses when you feel yourself sinking down into another realm and you forget about everything. Maybe that's what I was looking for, romance. These days though, would I have to ask if I could kiss her? Twenty years ago I didn't ask. A couple of times, in nightclubs, I remember walking up to women I didn't know, pulling them toward me and kissing them. Then I got their telephone number. I was arrogant back then, but these women did not seem to mind my kissing them.

In the parking lot I asked Ingrid if she wanted to get together again. As she got into her Jetta, she told me to email her.

That night I emailed Ingrid and we agreed to meet at a billiard parlor to play pool. Now I was convinced that she wanted to hook up with me. I wasn't sure, though. I would have to ask her what she wanted—what she expected. I would be completely honest with her. I'd tell her right from the beginning that I didn't want a divorce. If we were going to have an affair, we would have to be discreet. We would meet once a week—at her place. We'd go to movies or to lunch or we'd play pool or go for long walks in beautiful natural settings where I'd point out red-tailed hawks and red-winged blackbirds and then we'd go back to her apartment where we'd make wild, passionate love. I just knew that she would awaken that physical hunger that curled deep down within me like a lynx. But I didn't even want to get into that yet. I had to stop myself from going down that road. I was still obsessing about kissing her, indulging in and enjoying that. I'd fall asleep thinking about it and wake up with the feel of her lips on mine.

In class, she passed in a personal essay telling a story about her discovery, when she was in high school, that her father had a daughter with another woman. She called it "The Secret." Her mother already knew about it. It seems her mother and father had decided to tell her just to get it out in the open because Ingrid went to school with this other daughter and Ingrid's parents were afraid she would find out from the girl or from friends. Ingrid talked about how unnerving it was to be sitting across from her father while he confessed to her. Ingrid had been angry at him. "I wanted to send him to his room," she said in her paper.

I wondered if now she somehow subconsciously wanted to act out the same scenario with me. We would have a child together, and then years later, I would have to tell my sons about it. It would create a kind of cosmic balance. But no, that was silly, ridiculous of me to even think of; moreover, I could never raise such an idea with her. Maybe years later when we had been lovers for a long time—lovers like Chopin and George Sand, or Spencer Tracy and Katharine Hepburn. Ingrid and I would meet once a year or so at a remote resort in the mountains in Switzerland. Little Ingrid would gather flowers as Ingrid and I watched from the deck while drinking hot chocolate.

Anyway, it was quiet in the afternoon in the pool hall. She wore a pair of jeans, clunky sandals with heels, and a white tank top that accentuated her breasts and left her mid-section bare. She had a ring in her belly-button. I asked what she did to keep in shape. I blew my nose and put my hankie in my pocket.

"I like to kick-box," she said.

"Kick-box?"

"Ya, they have kick-boxing at the club I belong to and I practice two or three times a week—just for fun really."

I wondered how long it would take her to put me down on the canvas. I thought I would do okay with my fists, deflecting her blows and even if she got a few shots in, I could take the punches. It would be the kicks that would get me—kicks to the ribs probably. I saw myself toppling to the mat and looking up through blurry eyes at her. "Professor," she'd call, "are you all right?"

I asked what kind of music she liked.

"Dance music," she said. "I like to go to clubs in Boston—Avalon, Landsdowne's, the Zone. What kind of music do you like?"

I told her I had just bought an Al Green CD, but I knew the minute I said it, I'd have to come up with someone more recent. She wouldn't know who Al Green was. Who did my sons like? "I like Tool," I said, hoping she wouldn't ask me for a song title.

She knocked a low ball in the side pocket. "Really?" she laughed.

So I was engaging in various forms of deception already. I was deceiving my wife and family and I was deceiving Ingrid. I was beginning to dislike myself.

I had to talk to my friend Jack about it. I met him at a bar in Beacon Hill called The Sevens.

"You better be careful, you asshole," he said. He was smiling when he said it and I could see he was envious of me. We had been talking about politicians like Bill Clinton.

"Women throw themselves at those guys," he said. "They're like groupies; they follow those guys around."

We were drinking Harpoon Ale. We were on our second pint.

I was thinking that we men are weak when it comes to beautiful women. Jack was weak; I'm weak; Clinton, Spitzer, Edwards, all of us. I suddenly wondered if I looked as old as Jack. He had a bald spot and his hair was thin on top. His beard was overrun with gray and white strands. But it's not the looks, right? It's the power.

"I've said no to a couple of girls," I said to Jack. I sneezed. I'd had this damn cold for over a week.

"Yea, when? To who?" He pushed me off my stool.

I bumped into a woman who was sitting with her two women friends. All three were in their twenties. She shook her head and made a face at her friends. She could see I was just another stupid obnoxious guy.

"The other thing," Jack said, "is that this young girl probably doesn't see you the same way you see her. You might think she's attracted to you, but is she really? She's probably just interested in meeting you for coffee or friendship. You're this older guy who is kind of interesting, but she probably hasn't even thought about getting involved with you."

I could see myself in the mirror behind the bar. I looked good for my age. I wasn't fat. I had hair and it was mostly brown with some gray. From certain angles, in certain lights, with the right clothes, I could still look good. Who did I think I was fooling? Jack was right. She wasn't really attracted to me.

"Anyway," Jack said, taking out a pack of Marlboros, "it's a mid-life crisis."

"Gimme one of those," I said, grabbing for the cigarettes before he put them away. We pulled at the pack and two of them went flying into the circle of women.

The one I had bumped into crushed the cigarettes in one hand and crumbled them into an empty glass. She was overweight or maybe she was a weightlifter. It was hard to tell. She was wearing sweats and high tops.

"You are so strong," I said to her. "You are like Wonder Woman."

She turned back to her friends. Jack handed me a cigarette (we'd have to go outside to smoke it) and I thought about Marlboro Country transported to Sweden—Ingrid and I riding horseback, rounding up reindeer. "You're right," I said to Jack. "It's a mid-life crisis. I'm permanently pissed off because of my lousy career. I keep writing but nothing changes. I still end up in these stupid temporary adjunct teaching positions. I only have the one novel published. I've worked at six different schools. You know, I was thinking of trying to get a PhD a couple of years ago, but when I applied to the programs and they asked what kind of research I wanted to do, I couldn't come up with anything."

"You're just a lazy bastard," Jack said.

"I need a break," I said, as we walked back into the bar. I signaled the bartender for another beer. "One big break is all."

"There's no such thing," Jack said.

I pushed him as he picked up the pints off the bar and he spilled some beer onto his gray cotton shirt.

Wonder Woman looked at us with disgust.

That night I sent Ingrid an email asking her to meet me for coffee at Jake's the next morning. I got there early and read the local paper. Someone had published a bunch of emails between local politicians. I wondered if I should be careful with emails. Ingrid showed up late. She had her hair up and was wearing a white shirt and beige slacks. She looked very crisp.

"You live near here?" Ingrid asked without a touch of irony.

"Not far," I said. "Would you like to see where I live?" It wasn't supposed to go like this. I didn't want to bring her to my house. The neighbors, my wife's friend who lived down the street, who knew who might see us? That wasn't the least of it. My wife was so goddamn observant she'd know we'd been there. And she'd be able to tell from my guilty behavior something had happened. I'd be like the dude in "The Tell-Tale Heart"—crime written all over my face.

"That would be nice, ya," said Ingrid.

She followed me. As I drove, I considered lies for the neighbors, lies for my wife. I couldn't come up with anything believable. I parked in the driveway. She parked out front. I felt like a real estate agent. I was just showing an interested buyer the house. Maybe that's what I would tell people. Or maybe I could say I was tutoring a student. Ingrid walked down the driveway and we went in the back door. I glanced around at the houses on the street. I didn't see anyone. I had decided I would give Ingrid a tour. Maybe nothing would actually happen. I would just show her the house and then she would leave.

We got as far as the living room, where we fell onto the couch. The first kiss was good and long and smooth. It was a ticket to another domain, just as I'd anticipated, but I felt like we'd just gotten started when she grabbed my belt buckle. So this is the way it is these days, I thought and stood to strip. She stripped too. Her body was fine—she was in twenty-two-year-old shape—her skin tight on her muscles. She was ready for me when I entered her too and although I was anxious, I was hard, and I wanted her enough to overcome my anxiety.

I felt myself falling into her and I closed my eyes. I should have kept them closed I guess, but I worried I'd come too soon, so I opened them and looked down at her face and the oddest thing happened. It was as if I were looking at an entirely different person. Her head seemed suddenly too big, her face square and distorted, misshapen like a warped melon. She was grimacing a bit and there was a look of both fear and submission in her eyes. I felt like I wasn't seeing straight and I shook my head to clear the cobwebs and looked again. Where was the beautiful girl I'd been obsessed with? I sneezed and came suddenly, prematurely, and I felt my penis retreating. I pulled out.

She looked at me, confused. "Did you come?" she asked.

I nodded. "Yes, I'm sorry," I said. "I guess I was nervous. I didn't really expect this to happen so soon." I couldn't look at her. I found my pants, pulled out my hankie and blew my nose.

She sat up and grabbed her clothes and held them in front of her. "Where is the bathroom?" she asked.

A few minutes later I walked her out to her car. She got in and I gave her a quick kiss with the door open. "I'll email you," I said. As she drove off I took a look around the neighborhood. It was quiet. I listened to the mockingbird make fun of me for a moment.

It wasn't until I was taking a shower that I realized I hadn't even used a condom. I had one in my wallet, but it had happened so quickly I just forgot about it. God, that meant if she had anything wrong with her, I could get sick and I could give it to my wife. Jesus, today, she could even have AIDS. She might have it without knowing. She could be a carrier. Plus, she could actually get pregnant. I didn't even know whether or not she had used any protection or if she was on the pill. Then another thought occurred to me. What if she was already pregnant by someone else and she had just set me up so she could say the baby was mine and then she could get U.S. citizenship or even blackmail me? Shit, I was such an asshole. I couldn't even believe I had brought her back to the house. That wasn't the plan at all. What happened to the long, romantic kisses?

Then, too, I couldn't understand what happened with the way she looked to me—in that instant when I opened my eyes and looked down at her face. Was it my problem or was it hers? Had I been projecting some kind of image onto her for months? The one trait I had I thought I could trust was my vision. I saw people and things as they were. I could tell what people were like. Even there it looked like I was deficient. God, I hated myself. I really just should take myself out, drive my car into a stone wall— give my wife and kids a break. Then they could hook up with someone else. Someone they deserved. It was obvious that I had to talk to someone about this. I'd have to meet Jack for a drink but I couldn't do it tonight. It would have to be tomorrow night. Tonight it would have to be business as usual at home.

Dinner went along okay although my wife did ask if anything was wrong twice. It's amazing the way you can sit and have a conversation with someone at such times and appear to be normal when all these thoughts are crowding together in your head, and at the same time you are aware of it, the absurdity of it. I told her it was this cold—it was getting worse instead of better.

"Maybe you should get to bed early," she said.

After dinner I was clearing the table when I dropped one of the wine glasses on the floor and it shattered. It was the oddest feeling. It was as if I couldn't really feel the glass in my hand. I stood there and opened and closed my right hand, touching my thumb and my fingers together. There was this funny tingling sensation. I realized I felt it in both hands. I never dropped glasses. I had worked in restaurants and bars in my twenties and I was still careful about the way I handled china and glassware. I did feel really tired. I decided to go to bed after dinner.

I conked right out and slept well for the first time in months. I wasn't surprised that I felt kind of groggy when I woke. When I got up though, there was this numb feeling in my feet and I kind of shuffled when I walked. My wife had already gone to work. She left a note in the bathroom saying she didn't want to wake me. I picked up my toothbrush and dropped it and picked it up again. I had a hard time unscrewing the cap from the toothpaste, and it was difficult to squeeze the toothpaste out of the tube. My hands felt like I had mittens on them. I figured maybe it was some weird flu or virus. I went back to the bedroom and called into school and told them I'd be staying home. I had this sensation that I was slurring my words. My mouth didn't quite work the way it was supposed to. I climbed back into bed and fell asleep.

A few hours later I woke. It was hard to push myself upright. I was okay mentally, but my body felt like it was full of water. I shuffled downstairs. I had to check in with Ingrid. I turned the computer on. Everything was a struggle. My fingers were stumps without joints. I could barely get them to press down on the keys. There was a message from Ingrid. "Why haven't you emailed me or called? I don't know what you think you're doing," she wrote. "You're messing with my emotions. Do you want to be with me or not? I need to know where you stand right now. You're not being fair to me. I think I need to talk to someone about this: a counselor. I don't want to get you in trouble but I feel really confused."

Email may be fine for notes and correspondence but it is a terrible vehicle for personal communication. It's even worse than the phone and the phone isn't great. At least on the phone you can hear the tone of someone's voice. Email has no tone and although it is instantaneous in transmission, it may take hours, even days to get a response. You just have to wait. I called Ingrid's number. The recording was a guy's voice saying no one was available to come to the phone, please leave a message. I hung up. Did she live with a guy? I had to talk to her. I had to get to her before she spoke to a school counselor. Shit. This whole thing was spinning out of control. It took me forty-five minutes to get dressed. Getting my socks on and lacing my shoes was the hardest part. I had to pull my legs into the right position. My feet kind of flopped and I didn't seem to have the strength to pull my socks over my toes. When I tried to tie my shoes, I fumbled with the laces. They kept slipping out of my fingers. I pulled my jacket on but I couldn't get it zippered. I finally just left it open.

I was okay driving for the most part. The clutch was hard to push in and shifting was difficult. I had to really concentrate to keep my hands closed around the steering wheel. I drove slowly so I wouldn't have to brake in a hurry. It was around one o'clock by the time I got to school. I thought I might be able to catch Ingrid in the cafeteria on the third floor of the Humanities building. I knew she usually went there for lunch. I parked in the parking lot underneath Humanities. I made the mistake of trying to walk up the stairs. I kept having to stop, I was so weak. A young guy actually asked me if I needed help and I let him help me up the stairs. I searched all over the cafeteria but I couldn't find her. I barely had enough energy to make it home.

"This isn't a cold," my wife said that night. "I'm bringing you to the hospital."

I just nodded. She was obviously right. We went to the emergency room. A couple of hours later I was telling my symptoms to a neurologist. She said I had something called Guillain-Barré. "It's also known as polyneuritis," she said. She attached me to a machine that confirmed her diagnosis.

"Sometimes a cold or flu gets into your central nervous system and muscles," she explained. "That's what has happened to you. The good news is that it will pretty much go away eventually. Have you been under stress? It is sometimes stress-related." The doctor looked at my wife, then back at me. "You may be in bed for a couple of weeks depending on how much your symptoms progress. You'll have to let us know how you feel. Sometimes people get so weak, we need to help maintain their heart for them. Usually though, it doesn't get that serious. You will probably just need to spend a couple of weeks in bed and then you will start to regain your strength. You'll have to be patient though. It may take six months or more before you will feel really good again. Most people get back to 80-90% of their strength. You may lose some manual dexterity, but you should be able to function normally."

She checked her watch. She looked tired, my doctor. "There is no treatment," she said. "As soon as you feel you are able to work, you should return to work. You'll just have to rest until then." She smiled.

"I can go home?" I asked.

"Yes," she said, standing up. "Make an appointment to see me again in ten days and call me if you get any weaker."

We got home a little before ten. I called my boss's home number and told her what the story was and she said she would get a substitute for me, not to worry about it, to just get better. I listened to her voice to try to tell if she had heard from Ingrid, apparently not. So it seemed like

I was all right as far as work went. I'd just stay home and rest and get better. I'd get hold of Ingrid and tell her we couldn't see each other anymore. It would be painful but it would all work out and everything would still be intact. My job, my marriage, my life.

My wife stayed home with me the next day. She was very solicitous, making me tea, plumping my pillows. The phone rang around noon and my wife answered it.

"It's Ingrid," my wife said, handing the phone to me. "She says she's a student."

I was lying on the couch.

My wife wasn't quite sure what to make of it. She stood at the end of the couch for a moment, staring at me.

"Hi," I said. Ingrid was actually whimpering into the phone. My wife walked out of the room. Ingrid wanted me to come and meet her. She was at the health clinic. She wanted to know if she should get a morning-after pill and she was thinking of seeing a counselor. If I could just come and meet her and talk to her, that's all she wanted. She was confused, she said. "I need your help," she sobbed.

I told her I would get there as soon as I could but that it would take me a while. I put the phone down and pushed myself to a sitting position. Immediately I fell back. I wasn't going anywhere. My wife was back. She sat on the couch beside me.

"Maybe you should tell me what's going on," she said. She wouldn't look at me.

So I confessed. I confessed and begged forgiveness and absolution. I think if I hadn't been sick she would have given me the heave ho, but as it was, she pitied me, poor pathetic creature I was. She told me she wanted me tested to make sure I hadn't caught any sexually transmitted diseases. She told me I'd be sleeping on the couch until she decided different. I nodded and hung my head.

That afternoon I called Ingrid but I got the answering machine again. Finally I decided to send her an email. "I'm sorry, Ingrid," I said, "but I'm sick. I have something called Guillain-Barré syndrome. It isn't contagious. I can't come into school and see you or help you. I think it's a good idea for you to see a counselor. I don't mean to play with your emotions. I was a fool to think we could get involved casually. We really shouldn't see each other anymore." I hit *send*.

I called my boss and told her I would be out for at least two weeks. She told me not to worry. When I hung up I felt better for a couple of hours. It was going to be all right.

Then two hours later my boss called back. She said she had heard from the Counseling Office that a first year student, a student in one of my classes, had filed a complaint against me for sexual harassment. She asked if there was any merit to the charges. I told her that we had seen each other outside of class socially but that there wasn't any sexual harassment. "I see," my boss said. I could hear her sigh on the other end of the phone. "In that case

I think you should take the rest of the semester off and then look for a job elsewhere." She hung up. I thought of calling her back to argue but really, I didn't have a leg to stand on.

Two weeks later I was back on my feet, but I had lost ten pounds, and I wasn't fat to begin with. I was meeting Jack at the Sevens for a beer. I had seen the doctor earlier that week and she told me that weight loss was normal. I still felt weak but at least I was able to get around. I felt like I'd been in a kick-boxing match and I'd lost a twelve-round decision. Ingrid had emailed me that she was sorry she filed a complaint against me. She had told the counselor she wanted to drop it. She had taken a morning-after pill so she wasn't worried about getting pregnant. Meanwhile I had been tested for AIDS and two or three other sexually transmitted diseases; the results were all negative. Both Ingrid and my wife were happy to hear this. I was still sleeping on the couch.

I got to the Sevens bar early. I ordered a pint of bourbon while I waited. In the mirror I saw a wiry old guy with grayish brown hair. When he raised his glass to drink, his hands trembled.

Jack came up behind me. He gave me a double take. "What the hell happened to you?" he said.

I cackled and wiped the beer off my mouth with my sleeve.

PART TWO

ON AN ISLAND IN THE MOST BORING TOWN IN AMERICA

Rob Dugan rubbed his neck—stiff from searching for jobs at Monster and Hot Job. Now he was staring at the calendar that he had as a screensaver. Alex had Boy Scouts in the afternoon. Mandy had ballet. Julia had chorus that night. Nothing scheduled for Rob Dugan: unemployed for eighteen months. He never thought he would be out of a job for this long. The energy was slowly draining out of him. "What a loser," he said to his reflection in the monitor.

Plus, Julia was *not* the jazz singer he married; instead she was a secretary at the elementary school down the street where she did not make enough to cover their bills. And, and! His kids acted like little snobs who expected life to be a series of holidays and birthdays with endless presents and vacations ("Can we go to Disney World?"). The house was half renovated—they had to let the contractor go. The kitchen had an island in the middle at which he was now sitting, but one wall was unpainted sheetrock with a row of unfinished cabinets on the floor. And Milton was the most boring town in America. Rob shook his head. That's what an article in the local paper had recently claimed. According to the article, the average age in Milton was fifty-five. Half the residents were retired. It was the safest town in Greater Boston. It had no industry, no restaurants and no bars. Unemployed in the most boring town in America, ugh!

Until a year and a half ago, Rob had sold information on printing technology to computer companies. He flew around the United States and made presentations to clients. Because he reviewed high-tech equipment, companies like Dell and Canon and Apple were always giving him new toys. He had three computer systems in his house. Eighteen months ago, they had been cutting edge. Today Rob was going to take a three-year-old MAC to a place that bought used equipment for cash. He wondered what he'd get for it. Not much, he knew that. Three hundred maybe. Whatever, he needed it. He was broke and the bills were stacked on the desk in the den. He and Julia had already tapped her mother and his father for loans. The grandparents continued to pay for the kids' activities and clothes but no more hand-outs from the parents for Rob and Julia.

Two hours later, at 11:30 on a Saturday morning in February, Rob lugged the MAC from the office in the den through the kitchen. Julia was in the initial stages of baking spinach lasagna. Rob looked at her standing at the counter layering the noodles with spinach and cheese. Did she still have a nice body? She was really thin. Thin like his hair—what was left of it.

"I'm off," he said.

"When will you be back?" she asked without turning around.

"Sometime tomorrow if I get lucky and pick up a girl while I'm out, otherwise I should be back in a couple of hours." Rob was thinking he might find a bar and have a beer after he sold the computer. He kicked the door open with his foot. February—it was like, *winter, be over already.* He propped the computer against the Honda Civic, opened the door and sat it in the passenger seat. He put the seatbelt around the monitor to keep it from moving. "Buckle up for safety," he said. He went around the other side and got in and closed the door. Then he sat with both hands on the wheel. The Civic had 91,000 miles on it. There was a thumping sound that came from the right rear wheel when he applied the brakes. Could he afford to get it fixed? No way. Like most other problems he was facing, there was nothing he could do about it. He was unemployed, broke and impotent. Not sexually impotent (although there wasn't much going on in that part of his life either). He was impotent when it came to changing his situation. He sat for a minute without moving. "Warp 4, Mr. Sulu," he said, turning the key.

"I need coffee!" he proclaimed a few minutes later when he stopped at the light at the corner of Morton and Blue Hill Ave. He pulled into the Dunkin Munch. He got out of the car and took his keys out to lock it up when he noticed a reflection in the window of a guy in a black stocking cap with an afro sticking out the sides and then he felt something hard digging into his back and bad breath on his stiff neck.

"Okay my man, take that fat wallet of yours and give me what's in it."

So this was it. His heart began punching his chest from the inside. He was going to die in the parking lot of a Dunkin Munch before he had even gotten his coffee. He thought of Obama. He considered telling the robber he had voted for him. Then he thought of Rodney King being beaten in L.A. and the white census worker who had been set on fire just down the street twenty years ago. Rob held his trembling hands up in the air. He felt the anxiety ripple through him. "Twelve bucks," he said over his shoulder. "That's all I have. My credit card isn't even any good. It's maxed out." He felt like apologizing. *I'm sorry I don't have more money to give you.*

Rob felt the guy step away from him. "What are you telling me? You don't have no money?"

Rob turned around. His hands were really cold. "Twelve bucks," Rob said. "That's all." He was looking at a big guy—well over six feet with a wide body to boot.

He had an old army jacket on that made him look even bigger. His head was as round as a bowling ball. It was topped with the stocking cap. On his hands, wool gloves with the fingers cut off the ends. His right hand held a gun, a nine millimeter it looked like, pointed at Rob's heart, but when Rob looked into his assailant's eyes, he could see that they were red and rheumy. This dude was drunk. He was even rocking a little on his feet. And his eyes didn't look threatening. Instead, they looked nervous. The big guy glanced around the parking lot as if he were suddenly afraid of being caught. *This guy is not going to shoot me*, Rob said to himself. He took a deep breath. He breathed out and smiled. Rob had a smile that reassured and relaxed people. He had often relied on it in his presentations when he was nervous or didn't know what to say.

The big guy pulled his head back, confused. "What you smiling for?"

"I was thinking that if you shot me, my wife and kids would get some insurance. Are you going to shoot me?" Rob could hear his voice was wavering.

"Nah, man, I ain't gonna shoot you." The big man lowered the gun.

"I have an idea. How about this car?" Rob held up the keys. "Could you use a car?"

"That piece of shit. Man I wouldn't be caught dead in that."

"There's a computer in it," Rob said. "Do you want that? You could sell it."

"No, no I don't want no com . . . what I'm gonna do with that?" The big man put the gun in his coat pocket and crossed his arms. "Shit!" He furled his heavy brows.

Rob looked into his eyes. Was he crying? What the hell was going on here? "Hey," Rob said. "Let's go in and have a cup of coffee. I'll give you ten bucks and we can warm up." He was sure that if he got into Dunkin Munch, he'd be safe. He put his keys in his pocket and rubbed his hands together. He started walking quickly toward the Dunkin Munch. At least he wasn't stuck. He was doing something—taking a risk. This was definitely not boring! Rob looked back and saw the guy watching him. "Wait up, man," he said. He was breathing heavily when he caught up to Rob at the door. "I'm already outta shape," he said. "I was in pretty good shape in the joint but I been out three weeks and I just been hangin out here and at the Little Brown Jug." He bobbed his head at a nondescript bar diagonally across the intersection.

Rob nodded in understanding. "What were you in jail for?"

The big guy smiled. "Grand larceny, breaking and entering, possession. They give me two years in Walpole. They would eat you alive in there man." He seemed to say this with a certain amount of pride.

Rob took a deep breath, held the door and the guy shuffled in. He took a seat at the window. "How do you like your coffee?" Rob asked over his shoulder as he approached the counter. Five minutes ago he was being held up; now he was safe, ordering a coffee. How weird was that? He saw that his hands were shaking.

"You botherin this man, Willie?" asked a guy behind the counter. "If he's been botherin you," he said to Rob, "I can call the police."

Rob hesitated for a second. Did he want to tell the police what had happened? Get the guy locked up? Sent back to jail? He should. But he didn't want to. The guy had just gotten out and what had he done? Attempted robbery? Rob put his hand on his chest to feel his heart. He was okay. "Bothering me? No way," Rob said. "I was trying to convince him to kill me, but he wouldn't go along with it."

The Dunkin Munch man laughed.

"Medium regular for me," Rob said.

"Willie likes it black," the counter man said, handing two cups to Rob. Rob paid him and carried the cups to stools near the window. He put his coffee down and put the change on the counter in front of the big guy—Willie. Willie was sitting on his hands, leaning forward, his head down between his big shoulders. Rob looked closer. He was sniffling. There were tears striping his cheeks.

Willie pushed the money back toward Rob. "I cain't take that man. You got a family to feed. What kinda fool you take me for?" he blubbered and his whole body shook. "I cain't even rob nobody right, man. I'm a fool."

Rob patted Willie on the back. So Willie was a loser, just like him. Rob looked over his shoulder at the guy behind the counter—a young Hispanic guy in his twenties. He had an intelligent face. What was he doing working here? Maybe he had gotten laid off from a good job. Maybe they were all in the same boat. They could form a support group.

The counter man smiled and shook his head. "Hey, Willie," he said. "Don't be blubberin in here man. Take it outside. People don't like to listen to that."

"Lemme use the head first," he said. He took his coat off and draped it on a stool.

Rob could see the gun sitting in the side pocket of the coat. He looked over at the guys behind the counter. They were busy. Rob reached into the pocket, took the gun and put it in his own jacket pocket.

When Willie returned, he put his jacket on, picked up his coffee and walked outside. Rob followed him out into the parking lot. Willie turned to Rob suddenly, stepped forward and put his arms around him. Rob didn't know what he was doing at first but then he realized he was being hugged. Rob brought his right hand up to Willie's waist. He held his coffee out to the side with his left. He didn't want to spill it. His right hand covered the gun in his jacket pocket. He could pull it out and hold it on Willie. Turn the tables. Did he really even want a gun? He could shoot himself with it that night when Julia went to chorus.

Willie stepped away. He wiped his eyes with one of his hands. "I'm sorry man," he said. "I got to do something different. I'm gonna take classes, man. Get my GED. Then I can get a real job."

Rob held out his right hand and Willie shook it. "That's what I should do," Rob said, "take classes." Willie smiled and looked away. Rob wondered what he was thinking. Stick around and try another robbery? Well, he wouldn't have a gun anymore and maybe that was a good thing. Maybe Rob was doing him a favor.

"I have to go," Rob said. He walked back to his Civic and got in. Willie shuffled up beside the car. Rob turned the key and rolled down the window.

"You-all come back and see me," Willie said. "Next time, I'm buyin."

Rob smiled and waved as he drove off.

The guy at USED DOT COM hooked up the computer and turned it on. "Nice," he said. He told Rob he could sell the MAC on commission for, say, $500, or he could give him $350 right then for it. Rob was thinking that Willie should have taken the computer and brought it here. "I'll take the cash," Rob said. The place was a mess—computers piled up everywhere. There was no one else in the store. The guy went into a room in back. Rob now had the gun in his front pocket. He had his hand around it. He wondered how much cash the dude had back there, maybe a few thousand. Willie had called himself a fool. Rob felt like a fool too but he hadn't always felt that way. He had grown up in the working class city just east of Milton—Quincy. He was one of the tough guys in high school. He and his friends had broken into a few houses and stolen cash, jewelry, guns. But one of his friends overdosed on cocaine and another was run over outside a bar in Boston. After that Rob decided he had to change his life. He went to UMass-Boston and took classes in computer science. That's where he had met Julia.

The Honda was parked down the street. Computer dude didn't know him. He'd hold the gun on the guy and get him to give up all his cash. Then he would tie him up. Rob could walk out with his pockets stuffed with money. He'd stop at Dunkin Munch and give Willie a hundred and return his gun. He could pay off a few bills and give some cash to Julia. She'd smile and throw her arms around him. He could feel the safety latch on the side of the gun. No way. He did not want to be that person.

Rob heard the noise of a door opening behind him. He looked over his shoulder. A woman had come in. The computer man reappeared. He held a pile of bills out. Rob folded the cash and put it in his wallet. He signed the receipt: Robert Brown. He wrote a fake address and phone.

Rob drove back the way he had come. He needed to give the gun back. At the corner of Morton and Blue Hill he pulled into the Dunkin Munch lot but didn't see Willie. "Wait a minute, I could turn it in. That's what I'll do."

He drove out Blue Hill Avenue, passing closely set brownstones, liquor stores with neon signs and iron gates. There were laundromats, a place that promised to cash checks, an unemployment office, and a West Indian store-front restaurant. Near the Milton line big colonial houses began to appear. As he drove into Milton, the houses grew brighter and better cared for. They seemed to require more lawn to sit on. Rob drove right by his house. The police station was less than a mile away. He took out the gun and wiped it off with his jersey. He pulled a paper bag out from under his seat and put the gun in it. Inside the station he told the sergeant at the desk that he had found a gun in the parking lot of the Dunkin Munch. He put the bag on the counter. The sergeant gave him a form to fill out with his name and address and phone number.

A few minutes later, Rob pulled into his driveway. When he got out of the car, he heard a mockingbird working out his identity crises on a branch of the birch tree in the yard. Maybe it would be an early spring. Rob looked at his watch. It was 2:30. Why hadn't Willie asked for his watch? It was worth a few bucks. Julia had given it to him for his birthday. Willie needed to take a class in robbery. Maybe they both needed to go back to school.

In the kitchen Julia was just pulling the lasagna out of the oven. The smell of pasta, tomato, garlic and basil made him blink and smile. He was suddenly starving. What the hell had he been thinking? He was ready to rob someone. He was thinking of shooting himself. He wasn't so bad off. He wasn't hanging out at the Dunkin Munch or the Little Brown Jug. He didn't have to rob people. He had a beautiful wife and two kids. He lived in a house in Milton.

"That took a long time," Julia said, putting the lasagna on the island in the center of the kitchen. She turned to him and smiled. "How'd you make out?"

"Great," Rob said. "I sold the MAC for $350. Oh and some guy tried to rob me at the Dunkin Munch. This was before I sold the computer. Plus I, uh, found a gun and dropped it off at the police station."

"You're kidding." Julia wiped her hands off on a dishtowel and stepped toward Rob and put her arms around him. She pulled her head back and looked at him quizzically. "You are kidding, right?"

Rob hung his jacket up on a hook on the back door. Rob stepped toward Julia and kissed her. "He gave me an idea. I'm going back to school."

Julia was looking at him skeptically. Rob could see she didn't really believe him. He pulled her to him and kissed her again.

Julia leaned back and smiled at him. After dinner he'd do a little brainstorming—make a list of classes he could take that would help him find another job. He glanced over Julia's shoulder at the calendar. Alex and Mandy were still out—Alex with the Scouts and Mandy at ballet. He unbuttoned the top button on Julia's jeans and looked at her face to gauge her reaction. She smiled. She was game. Still a good-looking babe, Rob thought, lifting her onto the island of the most boring town in America.

QUALITY TIME

The main thing was getting to see my dad. Going to the Patriots game was extra. My dad was a Pats fan big-time—hat, shirt, the works. It was Patriots versus Buffalo. Just to get my dad going, I said I was for Buffalo. This was a few years ago, before 9/11, when the Pats were good and Buffalo kept getting to the Super Bowl and losing. But, like I said, it wasn't really the game. It was my dad taking me. He had left my mom the year before and he was coming back up to New Hampshire from Boston where he was living with "the babe," as my mom called her, and he was taking me on this big outing to the game to spend some quality time together. I was still hoping he would get back together with my mom.

He brought the plane with him. It was one of those remote control jobs. He had it all put together with the batteries in, all set to go. We had about an hour at the house before we had to leave so we carried it down to the park to try it out. I was still mad at him for leaving us for the babe, but I have to say I was excited about that plane. I had put models together myself, some with my dad—we both liked planes. We built rockets together too and launched them at a park. So, I wasn't shocked when he brought this plane, but I was surprised. I knew he was trying to buy me off—so what. The plane was big—two feet propeller to tail. It was open cockpit with two sets of wings—one above the cockpit, one below.

After a couple of false starts we got it up in the air, circling above the field. I remember other kids standing there watching. It made a loud buzzing sound so people would look up if they were walking by. I was getting a feel for the controls. At first it seemed easy but then when I tried to land it, I almost lost it in the trees. "Hey," my dad said, grabbing the remote from me. "For Christ's sake, Tommy." He brought the plane in and landed it right in front of us.

"So," he said, "how's it goin? Everything all right?"

I just looked at him. "Are you still with the babe?"

"No," he said. "We split up."

"Why don't you come back?" I grabbed the remote.

"I'd like to," he said. "I have to talk to your mom about it. Maybe after the game." He checked his watch. "We better hit the highway."

I asked, "Could I take the plane with me?"

"What for?"

"I don't know. Maybe there'll be time to fly it, at the half."

He looked away. Normally I think he would have said no, but I could see that this time, I had him. In fact, I was wondering if I could get him to buy me a Patriots jersey—home colors.

At the house I put the plane and the remote into my backpack (the nose, the propeller and the wings stuck out the top). My mom was in the kitchen, jamming some pots and pans into the cupboard—making a racket. I kissed her good-bye. She was crying. She walked me out and told me to stick with my dad and then she told my dad to drive carefully. My dad was sitting in the jeep, tapping his hands on the wheel. I tossed the backpack into the rear seat, climbed in and pretended to put on my seatbelt as we drove off.

Back in those days they didn't really check what you brought into a game—at the gate I mean. The guys taking tickets took one look at my backpack with the plane sticking out and laughed. Ha, ha, ha, big joke. In the stands, I took the pack off and kept it in front of my seat.

It was a good game. The Pats always played Buffalo tough. At the half it was Buffalo 14, Patriots 10. I had this bet with my dad—if Buffalo was up at the half, we would try to fly the plane on the field. I don't think he thought we would have time, but after the cheerleaders danced around to the rock music that blared from the sound system, and some kids performed a series of flips, or flip flops, or whatever you call those circus tricks they do, the field cleared off, I looked at my dad and he nodded.

I was afraid the security guards would stop us, but they just shrugged when I took the plane out and put it on the field. One of them even said something nice like, "Whoa, that is cool." I taxied it from the end zone; it took off and buzzed up into the sky. It was a beautiful day—crisp and sunny, big cumulus clouds in shapes you could argue about. Kids gathered around me as I circled the plane about a hundred feet up. It was pretty noisy in the stadium, but you could still hear the buzz saw sound. I had control of it and it felt good.

I tried to think out how to bring it down—remember the way my dad had done it in New Hampshire. I made the circles smaller and pushed the lever down. It seemed to be coming in all right. I looked at my dad and he smiled. I wanted to land it in the middle of the field, facing toward us. Out the corner of my eye I saw the Patriots on the sidelines. I had to hurry it up. The security guards were clearing the field. I don't really know exactly what went wrong. The plane seemed to speed up. My dad tried to take the remote from me but I wrenched it back. Then the plane was coming right toward us. Kids were yelling and screaming. Someone yelled, "Hit the deck!" and a bunch of them went down on the grass. I turned my head away and closed my eyes. I didn't even see it hit the guy.

When I looked, this old dude was lying on his back on the ground with his arms out and the plane on the field just beyond him. His body was twitching and the plane was making that *ennnh…ennh* sound engines make when they're trying to go but can't. I switched off the remote but it kept making that sound.

The paramedics were there fast. They were on duty for the game, but before they got to work, they hesitated for a minute and stared. One of them kneeled down and took the guy's pulse. They argued about what they should do. Then they put him on the stretcher and loaded him into the van. Meanwhile, I could see kids were holding their stomachs—holding it back till the paramedics left. Then they burst out laughing. Most of the crowd didn't even seem to notice what had happened.

My dad was in shock. He couldn't even talk. I think he blamed me but he must have blamed himself too.

A couple of policemen and a security guy came over and took down a statement. They also talked to my dad. They said they would be in touch. My dad asked if there would be any charges. They got this helpless look on their faces. "I doubt it," one of them said.

I was trying to figure out what I would say to my mom. I wondered how she would feel about it. I didn't really know how to feel about it myself. As I rode home beside my dad I just kept trying to come up with what I would say to people. I settled on: "I lost control of a remote control plane and it hit an old guy in the head."

The police didn't press charges. The guy's family understood it was an accident. Plus I was off the hook with my mom; she blamed my dad. She said it was his fault for letting me take the plane into the game. She wouldn't have anything to do with him after that. They were divorced within a year.

That was ten years ago. I dream about that remote control plane often. In the dream I'm flying the plane. It's smooth sailing until I try to land it and that's when I run into a headwind that knocks me off-course. I see my mom and dad waving me in on a landing strip in a field. I'm having a hard time controlling the plane. In one version of the dream I crash into my dad. In another I crash into my mom. In the third version I hit both of them.

BODY SURFING

I had invited my sister, Virginia, and her husband, Leo, and their three children from New Jersey to celebrate mom and dad's fiftieth wedding anniversary. They, along with my parents, were coming for the weekend of the fourth of July. Frank and I had bought a house on the beach in Scituate when I got pregnant with Christine. We'd been trying to have a child for so long, we had just about given up. We had in fact begun looking into adoption—I was thirty-seven—but then, miracle of miracles, it happened.

It was a difficult delivery. I wanted to do it naturally, with as few drugs as possible. I wanted to experience it and I got my wish. Thirteen hours in the delivery room. My back has never really been the same, but I was so happy about the baby that I didn't care. And Christine was a beautiful healthy baby. I don't think there is anything to compare to it—the first sight of an infant—she'd been inside me for nine months and there she was with her head elongated from the forceps and the wisps of black hair and the violet eyes she got from Frank's side—she was so perfect. For the first few months, she kept me up, of course, but then she was cooing and sleeping, and crawling and walking with first words mixed in there. The older she got the more she came to look like me—her violet eyes were almond-shaped like mine. She had the same pouty mouth and heart-shaped face I saw in the mirror. She was different from Frank and me though—always smiling, giggling, a happy child. I took a six-month leave of absence from Dr. Perry's office where I worked as his secretary. Then I went back part time and put Chrissie in daycare. Dr. Perry let me work flexible hours. He was getting older and didn't put in a full week himself anymore. I thanked God daily for Christine's existence, for what she brought to my life. She made us a real family. I kept my part-time hours even when Christine went to elementary school so that I could walk her to school and meet her when school got out. It was the summer after fourth grade when we had the anniversary party for my folks. It was hard to believe that Frank and I had lived on the beach for ten years.

Mom and dad were staying at the house with us the weekend of the anniversary party. My sister Virginia and her husband Leo and their kids were staying at the Old Towne Inn in the center. We had eaten an afternoon dinner together at the Green Briar Inn where we had surprised mom and dad (Happy Anniversary!) and they had feigned surprise in return. Then we all went back to our house. It was four o'clock when we took our drinks out of the house and down to the beach where we sat on lounge chairs while the kids played down by the water. Virginia's kids were seven, nine and eleven—two girls and a boy. Christine was ten. The girls were playing with Christine, who was thoroughly enjoying herself digging in the sand. They were using plastic buckets to make a castle.

It was a beautiful day, hot and sunny with the sky that razor blue it only seems to be a handful of times a year. It was hot, nearly ninety, without a trace of haze. We were drinking Marguerites—one of Frank's specialties. He makes them with fresh limes. It was one of those rare times when I didn't feel stressed—I don't know, it always seems as if there is some reason for tension in my family—mom's upset at me or at Virginia or at Frank for something we said or did, or the kids are acting up. Anyway, we were just sitting there. It was mellow really. Time was passing slowly like those wispy cirrus clouds that began to form on the horizon, while the ocean caught cups of sunlight and the spray from crashing waves made us gasp with surprise. I was keeping my eye on Christine as I sat and talked with mom. Christine was a good swimmer but the waves that day were big. There had been a storm the night before and it was a private beach—no lifeguards.

Anyway, mom wanted me to show her the rooms upstairs. I had recently painted them and rearranged the furniture. I said to Frank, "We're going up; keep an eye on the kids."

"Sure," Frank said.

It must have been, I don't know, maybe half an hour later when mom and I came back. I looked out at the beach and it was deserted. It was so strange. Empty red and blue buckets overturned in the sand. I looked up the beach to the jetty. I wondered if maybe everyone had gone out there. Sometimes Frank took Christine out on the rocks. Near the jetty I saw three kids. I couldn't quite make out who they were. I remember thinking they could be Virginia's kids. Then I wondered where Frank and Christine were. I thought, *he must have taken her somewhere. Maybe she had to go pee and he took her up to the house.* I walked down to the jetty and it *was* Virginia's kids. I asked them where Frank and Christine were and they said they didn't know. I was worried at that point. I headed back to the house and saw Frank coming down to the beach. He was alone. He must have left Christine with mom and dad is what I was thinking. "Frank," I said, "where's Christine?"

"She's with the other kids," he said.

I remember looking at him then. He had had a lot to drink that day. He always drank more when my parents came to visit. "No," I said. "She isn't with the other kids."

"Well, I left her with them," he said.

"Where were you?" I asked.

"I, I went to the house," he said.

I was standing close to him. I thought I caught a whiff of marijuana. "You went to smoke a joint," I said. "You went to get high."

"No, no," he said, "I went up to the house to use the bathroom."

"Well, I'm going to check the house," I said. "Maybe Chrissie is with Nana."

"OK," Frank said. "I'll talk to the kids—they're probably playing hide and seek."

He smiled and it made me really angry. I wondered how in God's name we had ever gotten married. I mean did I know this man? Did I trust him?

I went up to the house, hoping Chrissie was with dad. Mom and I had left dad on the beach and maybe he had brought her back to the house. Dad was sitting alone in the living room reading the paper. He hadn't seen Chrissie, hadn't noticed her when he came up.

It was Frank who found Chrissie floating in the waves. She was right at the shore—"in a foot of water," Frank said. When I came back out he was trying to resuscitate her—pushing down on her chest and breathing into her little mouth. She looked like a doll—puffy and lifeless. That's when I lost it. I pulled him off, screaming from my gut. I pulled him off and began shaking her and when she didn't respond, I remember getting up and hitting Frank, calling him bastard, murderer, drug addict.

"Tommy said he'd watch her," was all he could say. He looked longingly at Tommy and at Linda and Ginny.

Tommy shrugged and said he was sorry. He started crying.

The girls said that Chrissie was playing with Tommy.

How could I blame Tommy? I hugged him and told him it wasn't his fault. He was just a kid after all.

My father had called an ambulance. They arrived fast and rushed her to the hospital where a team of doctors tried to bring her back. I guess they're sometimes able to do that. Not this time. I don't really remember much of it. I was in shock I guess. Dad was there and he took care of the details. Frank walked out of the hospital when they told us she was gone. I think he needed to get drunk. He didn't come home until early the next morning and he slept downstairs on the couch.

Dad was great. He stayed and arranged the wake and the funeral. I don't think I'll ever get over seeing her little body in that coffin. Her face was so placid and content. They had put a little make-up on her and I could see her going to her prom and graduating, getting married and starting a family. I just know she went straight to heaven. She was just one of God's little angels, Chrissie was.

There were media people, reporters, at the house and at the wake and the funeral. It was in the *Globe,* the *Ledger,* the *Herald.* It was on television too. My mother kept the articles. I couldn't read them. I never said a word to the reporters. I heard they found Frank at O'Grady's bar and asked him to make a statement but he was incoherent. My dad told the press we had nothing to say. We just wanted to be alone. I did get a lot of sympathetic calls and cards from neighbors and some from people I didn't know.

I blamed Frank. I needed to blame someone. I blamed my parents a little for the fact that Frank had to hide his smoking a joint by going into the house, but mostly I blamed Frank and from that moment on I just couldn't be near him any longer. I could not bear to look at him because every time I did I thought of Chrissie and his stupid selfishness—his weak need to get high and drunk. And I blamed myself too, it was my fault—like my mother says, I was the mother—I should have stayed down on the beach—you can't trust men to look after children—they are only men, is how my mother put it. Anyway, I couldn't stay with Frank anymore. A week after the funeral I told him to leave and he did. He didn't even seem surprised. He'd been sleeping downstairs. He'd stopped going to work.

He moved across town with an old high school buddy of his. I had to learn to live by myself. If I weren't Catholic I would've taken a bottle of pills the day of the wake. After that day I searched my soul for the sins I must have forgotten, for my selfishness, for my aimlessness, for where

I went wrong, what I did to deserve what happened, but I couldn't find the answer. I felt some guilt for Frank's drinking and smoking pot. I thought maybe I was not able to please him enough in the way he wanted. It was my fault he got high. I knew what he was like when I married him. I was over thirty and two years older. I was a little bit desperate, thinking of my biological clock. I wanted a child and a family and a home for the child so I compromised. Frank was not educated. He hadn't even finished high school. He was a carpenter who worked steady and I thought I could live with his faults. We liked the same music. Like me, he was a Dylan fan. I told myself it didn't matter if he drank and smoked dope. He was never abusive. In fact, I used to drink with him and although I didn't smoke pot, I never felt it was my place to condemn someone else. We'd met at church and I felt that was a sign. I didn't know then he only went twice a year.

It was Easter when we met. I was wearing a beautiful blue suit with a short skirt and heels and a white hat. I looked good. He had a tweed jacket on that looked a little worn around the edges and a white shirt open at the neck. He was tall and thin and he needed a haircut. I didn't think I could change him but I thought I could tone him down a little, spruce him up, soften the edges.

Two years after Chrissie drowned, Virginia was visiting with her kids. Virginia and I were in lounge chairs on the beach. Her two girls had gone for a walk along the shore.

It was a little cloudy that day, humid with a hint of fall in the breezes off the ocean. Tommy had just come up out of the water and was toweling off. He was thirteen and it seemed as if he had grown a foot in the past year. He was already taller than I was.

"Tommy has something he wants to tell you," Virginia said. "Go ahead," she said to Tommy, "tell her."

"It was kind of my fault," Tommy said.

I knew right away he was talking about Chrissie. It was never very far from my thoughts. Certain images floated at the edge of my vision—her in the water, Frank pushing on her chest, her at the wake.

"I said I'd watch her, like uncle Frank told me to," he hesitated.

"No one blames you," I said. "He was supposed to be watching her."

"But we went in the water together—Chrissie and me. We were body surfing. The waves were a little bit big and there was an undertow." Tommy looked at his mother.

"Keep going," she said. She was smoking a cigarette. I had been trying to get her to stop smoking but she just ignored me.

"We both rode this one wave and it pulled us under. It was really weird, like I was a pretzel being twisted underneath the water and I couldn't breathe. I thought I was going to drown and then I popped up and I looked around for Chrissie and I saw her. She was just a little bit farther out than I was. We were between the waves and another one was coming. Well I just swam as hard as I could for the shore."

"You mean you think you could have saved her?" The words just came out of my mouth.

"Yea, I knew how to—I had taken a class at the Y. I just panicked and wanted to save myself." His voice caught on the last word and his eyes filled with tears.

"Why didn't you tell me before?" I asked.

"I don't know. I guess I felt guilty."

"Okay," Virginia said, "you can go." She waved him off with one hand and he walked down toward the water. "He told me last weekend," she said to me. "He has an appointment with a therapist next week." She reached over and held my hand. "I'm so sorry."

I called Frank that night and met him for lunch the next afternoon. He didn't say much when I told him. He just nodded and looked out the window of the restaurant. Finally he said, "So, you're telling me it wasn't my fault?"

"No," I said. "I still blame you, but not completely. Maybe it could have happened even if we were right there. I'm not sure anymore."

He looked at me with those violet eyes, now encased in wrinkles. It was as if his eyes had sunk back into his head. "Well, Tommy shouldn't blame himself. He was only eleven. The thing was, I wasn't high. I was buzzed from the drinks and I ran up to use the bathroom. I tried to go in the water but it was too damn cold." He laughed and then stopped and his eyes welled up.

"Can we meet again?" I asked. I reached across the table and held his hand.

He shrugged and shook his head. I don't think he was saying no though. He was just shaking it off, commenting how awful the whole event was and how it didn't really change the fact that Chrissie had died. He mumbled something.

"Did you say something Frank?"

"I was thinking of a line by Dylan—something like: People don't live or die; people just float."

I looked at him sideways. "Chrissie drowned and she left us here, floating."

He nodded. He was staring out the window but I don't think that he was looking at anything. He needed a little time to absorb what I'd told him. I'd give him a little time and then I'd invite him over for dinner, just the two of us.

GETTING IN TROUBLE

It isn't being left home alone I mind. I was on my own for a long time in my life before I met my wife. What I mind is that she treats me like a child and hides the car keys on me when she goes out. Like a blue-footed booby, I'm grounded. And neither one of us is extinct—yet!

Plus, there are no Rice Krispies—what I always have for lunch. Decaf for breakfast. I don't go for all that *have a big breakfast* stuff. I'm six feet tall and I weigh 130. Every year I lose a little weight. Anyway, Ellen, my wife, is here in the morning if I need any help with anything, but she goes off to do her volunteer work at eleven at the museum or the damn church. She takes the bus. She cares more about those people than she does about me. That's obvious. The nurse comes by in the afternoon. Really I'm just alone for a couple of hours and the fact is, I don't go anywhere. I stick around the house, maybe work in the yard, rake or weed the garden. The paper boy, nice kid, always says hello, delivers the paper in the afternoon. Ellen comes back by three and we have tea together.

So at noon on this particular day of our Lord, whatever the hell day it is, I open up the cabinet to get the cereal and there isn't any—all gone. I figure I'll take the car down to the market. Why not? I spend the next forty minutes searching for the keys. If there's one thing I hate, it's looking for stuff I can't find. I swear I spend half my waking hours looking for lost, misplaced and forgotten items. I put my glasses down. Five minutes later I can't find them. I leave magazines in the bathroom and forget I left them there and go searching around the house, clomping up and down the stairs until I can hear my heart whomping against my chest like a bunny thumping its hind foot. I have to sit down and calm myself. Talk the bunny down to get my breath back. Sometimes I get lightheaded and have to lie down. Next thing I know I'm waking up two hours later and the nurse is sitting there knitting.

Some guys get sexy nurses. I get the knitting nurse, the overweight nurse, legs like stumps. Why I need a nurse I have no idea. All she has to do is dole out some pills I could as well take myself if they were labeled so I could read them. She takes my blood pressure (which I could do myself) and my temperature. Big deal.

I find the keys in Ellen's bureau in the top drawer under her underwear—the sexy underwear. Why would she have sexy underwear? She must have a boyfriend she meets at the museum or the church because she ain't wearing them for me I'll tell you that much.

I stuff my wallet in my back pocket and head out. It takes me a half hour to figure out how to get the car going. It's a new car, German, a VW Passat. Ellen just bought it. It has this remote with a key on it that doesn't even look like a key. I can't see the symbols on the remote and I guess I keep locking and unlocking the doors because I can't get them open. I finally get the hatch to pop and I climb in the car that way. It's a wagon with a hatchback. Can you tell me why they have to make these cars so small?

I can't get the key in the ignition. Finally, when I get the damn car going, it is barely moving, chugging down the street until I realize the emergency brake is on. That's the kind of mistake I hate to make. Maybe Ellen is right to hide the keys on me. I don't deserve to drive the car. I'm a goddamn menace to society and I ought to take the car up on the highway, bring it up to ninety and find a good tree. What the hell am I alive for if I can't drive myself to the store and buy some food?

I drive slowly and I know people are angry at me— hitting their horns and cursing, giving me the finger. I just smile and keep going. I have to read the signs and I need to get close to see them. I want to get onto Main Street and follow it to the four-way intersection and go right where that big rock is. I get to the four-way and by the time I make it through there I'm sweating because there is always a lot of traffic and no traffic lights. Why don't they put a light in? All these impatient, rude people get angry at me, but it isn't my fault. Americans don't respect their elders. I worked hard for forty years servicing machines at IBM and I deserve a little respect. Damn right I do.

I pull into the lot. I park at the back, facing out—less chance of getting hit by all the maniacs. I get out of the car and try to figure out how to lock it, hitting the buttons over and over until I just give up. There are bushes and trees just behind the parking lot. Birds are chirping away. They have the right attitude. They don't care about us. I see a cardinal, bright red with his black mask. He's perched in a maple whistling. Probably calling for his mate. He is a northern cardinal. See? I still remember some things. I'm not a complete idiot. I feel like a bird myself—spindly legs, sharp beak, bald head, beady eyes. You'll look like this if you live long enough.

Well, it is really nice out today. The sky is blue with wispy white puffs. I inhale. It should be fresh air but I can smell the exhaust and smoke from all the cars and it makes me cough. Why do people have so many cars anyway? The young couple across from us has three cars: two SUVs and a little two-seater that Mr. Dot-com keeps in the garage. They must be rich. They must be millionaires. He explained his business to me once and I didn't understand a word he was saying. I hear a horn and turn my head toward it and see a car waiting to get into the space I am standing in. What the hell am I doing in this parking lot? I look over the car and see the Star Market. My stomach grumbles. I remember. I came here to get some kind of cereal. I'm not worried. I'll remember when I get in the market and see the brands.

I trudge across the lot. By the time I get to the market I'm dizzy. I stop and take a few deep breaths. I pull a cart off the row and lean on it for support. Yeah I'm just like the rest of these old geezers—leaning on their carts as if they are walkers. If you pulled the cart out from under these people half of them would drop to the floor and croak. It's pathetic. I know where the cereal aisle is—it's near the fruit and vegetables. I turn down it. Now what was it? What did I want? I stare at the hundreds of boxes. Tigers, squirrels, bears and birds smile back at me. Some of the boxes are huge: Cheerios, Waffle Crisps, Grape Nuts, Cap'n Crunch, Fruit Loops. I used to like those. When I was a kid we ate everything. There wasn't any of this healthy food talk. I was always hungry. There were four kids in my family. My father was always complaining about how much we ate and how much milk we drank. He'd come home with gallons of milk and it would all be gone the next day. At school I would drink three cartons of milk and eat three lunches. What did it cost? Nothing, pennies, a quarter for lunch. I get a flash. It's a blue box

I'm looking for. Krinkles? No, it's snap, crackle, pop—Rice Krispies! I find them between the healthy granola and something called Kashi GOLEAN. What is that—Indian food? I pull a gigantic box of Rice Krispies off the bottom shelf. It feels so light. I shake it to make sure there's cereal in there. I'll probably die before I finish it all.

What else? Milk. How about bananas? I should have made a list. Ellen's a big list-maker. She makes multiple lists and compiles them into a master-list. Sometimes I get up at night and find her sitting downstairs scribbling: things to do, things to buy. I get in the fast check-out line. I pat my pants pocket. Thank God I brought my wallet. I reach in to pull it out but it gets stuck. I have too much junk in it. I should throw away all those cards and addresses and notes. I have to write down all the numbers and passwords so I can check them. All those numbers and passwords drive me nuts. I reach around with one hand and hold my pocket and pull the wallet out at the same time with the other. Quite the ordeal. Do I have any money? I have two bucks. Typical. I should get some money out of the friendly automatic bank. That's okay. I have a credit card. Of course I can't work the little credit card machine. I can't read it and need help from the cashier—a Middle Eastern woman wearing a scarf. She has a red dot on her forehead. That means she is a married woman. She's nice to me. She takes my card and runs it through the machine. The guy behind me is steamed. I'm holding him up. It's the fast check-out line and he is stuck behind me. The cashier, whose name is Amal, gives me the slip and I sign it. I take my bagged goodies and head for the door.

The sun is blinding. I'm halfway across the lot before I realize that I don't remember where the car is. The lot is not that big though. I can find it. Where do I usually park? A simple matter of deduction. I always park near the edges so I won't get hit; therefore the car is probably near the back or the sides of the lot. It's really gotten pretty damn hot since I went into the market. The heat makes it hard for me to think. I scan the cars. The sun shimmers off the metal. I'm a little woozy. I remember seeing some birds when I parked. A cardinal. What kind of car is it though? That's a good question. I reach into my pocket and pull out the keys and hold them out in front of me: VW. That's it. I walk to one side of the lot and head toward the back and I find it! A brand new VW Passat wagon. What a nice looking car! It's a shiny silver color. It doesn't take me long at all to get it open and get in but I'll tell you, by the time I'm sitting in the driver's seat, I am exhausted. My arm drops down and I feel a circular knob—just like on old cars. It is for adjusting the seat and I turn it back, relax and fall asleep.

When I wake up I check my watch. It's just after two. That means the nurse will be at the house looking for me. I've got to get back there. My shirt is wet. I feel my chin and sure enough there's drool. Yup, I drool when I sleep. What can I say? I'm a slob, a moron, a child. I'm lucky I didn't pee in my pants. In fact I check just to make sure. Nope, they're dry. Thank God for the little things. The other problem is that now I am really hungry. I haven't had lunch and that means my blood sugar is low and that is not good. It makes me nervous. My hands shake as I start up the car. I have to get home before the nurse calls my wife. I can feel my blood pressure building. I need pills to keep that down. I need pills to thin my blood so I don't have a stroke and I take a handful of other pills for who knows what else. My memory deteriorates when I haven't eaten and when I'm under stress. I would consider this a stressful situation. There's a cell phone in the glove compartment of the car but I don't know how to use it and even if I did, if I tried to use it while driving I would probably drive off the road so I figure, what I'll do is, I'll stop and call at a pay phone just to let the nurse know where I am. I want to call her before she calls my wife. There's change in the car. There's a pay phone at the gas station near the four-way and that's where I pull in.

I park the car beside the phone. It occurs to me that all gas stations look more or less alike. Sounds like the first line of a book. What was the name of that book? I put in a dime but don't get a dial tone. I put in another dime. Nothing. A nickel. I'm thinking maybe it doesn't work, but when I put in a third dime I get a dial tone. Thirty-five cents to make a local call! I start to dial but then I remember I have to dial the area code too. I am not a total fool. I hang up and put the money back in and dial again but I make another mistake. I hit the phone against the wall, hang up, re-insert the change and dial. The nurse picks up.

"Wilkens residence," she says.

"Hi, it's me," I say.

"Mr. Wilkens?"

"Yes, I went to the store. I'll be right back. I'm just a couple of miles away. I have the car."

"You're driving?"

"Yes," I say. "I needed to go to the store so I took the car."

"Well I've already called Ellen," she says. "She's on her way home. I called the police too. I thought maybe you wandered off. Why don't you just tell me where you are and we'll come and get you."

"Uh huh, well, I'll be home soon." I hang up.

I'll tell you something. Sometimes I just hate women. They worry too much. They make a big deal of everything. Okay, maybe I shouldn't have taken the car but I was hungry. I am a grown man. No, I don't have a license anymore. It was taken away by some idiot judge who blamed me for an accident I had no control over. I skidded through an intersection on an icy road and smashed into a motel. Big deal. Who did he think he was, pulling my license?

I find myself pacing, breathing heavily. *Calm down, take a deep breath*, I say to myself. *Walk it off and by the time you get home, you won't be angry anymore and you can have something to eat.* But as I'm walking I suddenly realize that it doesn't look very familiar. This must be a new neighborhood. The houses are huge! That's what drives me nuts, the way they are always changing everything. How is a person supposed to find his way around? I've been walking for about ten minutes when I remember I left the car at the gas station at the four-way.

Now I'm in trouble. I stop at the corner and grab onto the stop sign for support. What are my choices? I can try to retrace my steps to the gas station and get the car and drive home. It must just be only a couple of blocks from here. The problem is that I wasn't really paying attention when I was walking. I could probably knock on the door to one of these houses and use their phone. I still have all the numbers in my wallet. I reach back and pat my pocket. It's empty. Jesus Christ! It must be in the damn car. Or maybe I left it on the counter at the supermarket. What else can I do? I could just walk. I'm trying to remember which way I came from. I'm searching for an image. That's when I start to get the fear. It's really an irrational feeling that comes over me from time to time when I don't feel as if I am in control. It's a creepy feeling. I have to take deep breaths and focus just to keep myself from bursting into tears like a three-year-old. A kid on a bike stops beside me.

"You okay, Mr. Wilkens?"

I'm not sure who he is for a second, then I get an image of saying hi to him. He's the goddamn paperboy! "Tell you the truth, son," I say, "I'm not feeling so good."

"Do you want a ride?" he asks.

I look at his bike. It's an in-between size. Not as big as the bike I had when I was a kid but not one of those tiny trick bikes that some teens ride either.

"You sit on the seat," he says.

I climb on the seat, keeping one foot on the curb for support. This is one time it helps that I'm tall and thin. Soon I'll disappear—just like the blue-footed booby.

"You hold onto my waist," the kid says.

I put my hands on his hips and stick my legs out so my feet don't hit the ground. He pushes off with one foot and turns the pedal with the other. We swerve from side to side. I tap the pavement with my feet to keep us up and all of a sudden we're off—gliding down the street. What a great feeling! The old bird has got his wings back now. I'm flying just like I did on my bike when I was twelve. I'm smiling like crazy. I remember what it felt like to cruise with the wheels spinning beneath you and the wind in your hair. The street is all downhill—not steep though. We take the corner wide and the boy is pushing hard with his feet and pulling with his hands. He is one strong kid. I see my house! He pulls up onto the sidewalk beside the lawn and stops and the bike falls sideways and we both roll onto the grass. We're lying there laughing when Ellen and the nurse come out. Ellen has her hands on her cheeks. The nurse has her fists on her hips. They are both closing in on me. Oh boy, am I in for it.

NO EXPERIENCE NECESSARY

In the summer of 1985, I was painting triple-deckers in Roxbury, Massachusetts. I came up from Carol, Pennsylvania, which is where I grew up. People ask me where Carol is near and I just say, nowhere. Really, it's forty miles west of Philadelphia. What was I doing in Roxbury? Well, as my roommate, Janie, said to me, I was cherry—fresh off the farm and I didn't know any better. I came up to stay with my aunt while I found a job and my own place. I brought a thousand bucks with me, cleaned out my savings. Found a job through the classifieds: Painters, No Experience Necessary. I was the only female, worked with three guys. One of them knew what he was doing. He'd mix the paint and tell us where to go and what to do. He was an artist, he said, but made his money painting houses. It was slow, hot work in the summer. Did I care? Not when I was getting ten dollars an hour.

Janie I met when I answered another ad: "Woman looking for roommate to share expenses: $500 per month." It was the cheapest rate I saw in the paper. Now I know that was because of the location.

So there I was ten days after I left home, eighteen years old, living with Janie in Roxbury and making money. Roxbury seemed to be mostly, but not all, black and Hispanic. That didn't really matter to me because where I had come from there were no black people, no Hispanics either. You might think this would make me prejudiced but that's not the way it worked. I had no prejudice. The only image I had of minorities came from TV and movies and the news and I knew enough not to trust that.

Anyway, Janie was from the neighborhood. She worked at the cleaners on Washington Street. At night, Janie and me would go to this little hole in the wall bar called the Quarterdeck where they never checked IDs. The bar was owned by two white schoolteachers. I felt safe there even though most nights Janie and me would be the only white women in the place. The Puerto Ricans mostly kept to themselves. They would hang around a couple of the booths. The other booths would be filled with black men and women, and men would line the bar. Janie and me sat in stools down the end of the bar near the office.

One thing I found out fast was that people from the city tell you anything. A friendly woman named Willa May gave me advice on men: "Keep your eyes open honey—they be after you cause you a white girl and black men like to git them a white girl on their arm just to show the world."

I told her that boys weren't really ever interested in me. I'd always been heavy and I knew I was no beauty.

"Don't matter," Willa May said, holding up her empty glass and pointing to it. When she got the bartender's attention she said to him: "This time put Seagrams in it. I wanna see you open a new bottle. That ain't Seagrams in that bottle." She turned to me. "They always tryin to get over girl." She leaned back and looked me up and down. "You call yerself heavy? What do you call me?" She laughed.

Willa May outweighed me by fifty pounds, but she had curves. She had boobs the size of watermelons. Plus I had straight, dirty brown hair, freckles, and skin so pale I never went out in summer without a hat.

"These niggas like a woman of substance. Ain't that right Jerome?"

Jerome was Willa May's husband and he was about half her size. He had come up to the bar to order another drink. "That's right," he said, patting Willa May on the butt. He ordered a Seven and Seven and a Bud for me.

You have to understand that a couple of weeks before this I was in Carol, Pennsylvania working at George's Hardware in the strip mall. The other guys who worked there called me "the girl." I pretty much just covered the register. The men who came in would never ask me questions about what to buy or how to do things. I only had the job because George, the owner, lived next door to us. We lived on a small farm. We had a cow, some chickens, two horses and pigs. My dad worked part time at the post office and the rest of the day he'd spend working on the farm.

Nights I would hang out at "the rock," which was this place in the woods where all the high school kids would go to smoke and drink. Boredom was the main event in Carol, boredom and church. When I was a kid I believed. My daddy said you had to work at being a good Christian and if you didn't the devil was always waiting for you. Everyone, all the kids anyway, talked about getting out of town but what most of them got was pregnant and married and they never went anywhere.

When I was little, I liked it there. It was corn country and in spring and summer the air had that sweet country smell of hay and alfalfa. As a kid you could play by yourself. I could go down to the pond and fish, or I could throw stones, or catch frogs. There were redwing blackbirds and bullfrogs and foxes and raccoons and deer. But by the time I was in high school, nature bored me, I didn't care about my soul and I wanted out.

I figured Boston because I had an aunt from Boston who used to come down and visit us and she was everything I wanted to be. Tall and thin, she wore her hair back. She always had makeup on and wore short skirts that showed off her legs. She was a legal secretary and she always had a new car. She was my mother's sister. Talk about opposites. My mother was plain as milk. Momma was a homebody and she went around the house in her bathrobe until noon. My momma cried when I told her I was leaving and my dad told me to keep my eyes open. He had been to the city, he said, and it was like walking into the lion's den. My momma gave me a cross to wear around my neck, but the first thing I did when I got to Boston was to take that cross off and put it in my bureau.

So, as I was saying, Willa May was always telling stories. "Watch your back," she said to me, "you could end up like Willy. See that light-skinned nigga with no teeth—skinny one down the end of the bar? He wears them painter's pants like you all."

Willy wore his painter's pants without a shirt.

"A couple of years back," Willa May said, "he come here from Detroit. Walks in with a white linen suit, a cane, a what-you-call-it?"

"Panama hat," Matthew said. Matthew was standing right beside me at the bar.

"That's right," Willa May said, "Italian shoes, big motherfuckin smile on his face. You know what everyone like here—they all be friendly to him and he sets them up with drinks. Every time he buys, he flashes this wad of bills."

"All twenties," Matthew said.

Willa May had her hands on her hips. "We all see the roll and you know that nigga ain't goin nowhere. When he goes into the men's room, Matthew here and Andy and Russell follow him in."

"We didn't beat the boy," Matthew said. "We got him high on herb. And we give him a couple of valiums."

Willa May smiled. "When he comes out he can barely stand. Then Pat comes in. This is back when Pat looked good—when she was doin half the home-boys in this bar."

Matthew nodded and smiled.

"Pat puts her arm around Willy." Willa May put her arm around Matthew. "Then Pat starts buyin drinks with Willy's money. Buys a drink and pockets the change. After a while she takes Willy out to the alley. Willy comes back in zippin his pants and smilin."

Matthew laughed. "His hat and cane is gone and so is Pat."

"That's right," Willa May said. "Willy walks out the front and Matthew and Andy follow him."

"We rolled him," Matthew said. "Got a couple hundred."

"A week later the nigga comes back in," Willa May said. "His teeth are gone. He's wearin the same suit only now it's a mess. He ain't got no money and he done lost that uppity attitude. Meanwhile Matthew, Andy and Russell all come down with the clap. It hits us that Willy musta give Pat the clap an she give it to all these other niggas. So Matthew says to Willy, 'You betta git your ass back to Detroit boy.'"

"Now, you can see by the look on poor Willy's face he don't know what's happened to him. 'I ain't got no money now,' he says. 'I gots to stay put till I can save me some before I can go back home.' Then he says, 'Cain't none of you all buy me a drink?' 'None of us is drinkin man,' Matthew tells him, 'We's all on the penicillan.' That's when Willy laughed." Willa May laughed thinking about it.

"I woudda hit him," Matthew said, "but the mutherfucka didn't have no teeth. I felt sorry for him. So I says, 'Bartender, give this boy a beer.' Willy and me was friends after that. And don't you know that Willy been here goin on two years now?"

I bought a round for Matthew and Willa May and Jerome.

"Tell that story about Ann," Willa May said to Matthew.

"Nah..." Matthew smiled.

Willa May took my arm. "I know you a little bit afraid a Matthew cause he's so dark. Put your arm next to his."

She pulled me over next to Matthew. It was true. He made me look like a ghost.

"Even women of color sometimes afraid of Matthew. He looks like he's right outta the Congo. Don't he?" Willa May laughed.

Matthew was still smiling but his eyebrows were up. "Watch yourself girl," he said to Willa May.

"Honey," Willa May said to me, "you know Ann? You seen her in here with me. She's just about five feet tall. You don't want to git that girl angry. Am I right, Matthew?"

Matthew nodded. "When we was first livin together I come home once after bein out for two days and two nights. There's nobody in the house so I goes into the bedroom and falls asleep in my clothes. Few hours later I feel somethin cold on my throat. I'm havin trouble breathin. I open my eyes and there's Ann sittin on my chest with my .38 stuck in my throat. 'Where you been boy?' she say to me. I tole her, 'I'm sorry honey. I tried to call only there warn't no answer.' 'This ain't goin to happen agin is it?' she say. I say, 'No mam.' Okay. Two years go by and I run into this ole friend Sweeney and we end up out all night at the after-hours bars and throwin that dice. About nine in the mornin I roll my Buick into the driveway. I see Ann at the door. I just start to git outta the car and Ann shoots a hole right through the windshield. I jumps back in the car and worm down below the dash, back the car out and take off. An hour later when I stop shakin I give Ann a call from here. I say, 'Honey, can I come home now?' She says, 'You stay out on me agin I'll kill you.' I say, 'Yes dear.'"

We all laughed and laughed. They were funny stories. Now that I look back on them I guess I should've known that if I hung around long enough I'd end up one of those stories. My big mistake was having sex with Matthew. What happened was that Janie and me had gone back to Willa May's place one night after the bar closed and Matthew and me ended up in Willa May's bedroom. Willa May had passed out in the living room on the couch. To tell the truth I don't remember all that much of it. I was pretty buzzed. He was the first man I been with. Part of me wanted to say no and the other part wanted to get it over with. It did feel good when he kissed me. I liked the smooth feel of his skin and the way he smelled. It reminded me of home somehow—in spring when we'd turn the earth over to do the planting. I remember Matthew was mad at me. "Don't just lay there," he said. I tried to please him but I didn't really know what he wanted. Later, when he was getting dressed, he sat on the edge of the bed talking half to me and half to himself: "Oh man, I am in big trouble if Ann finds out about this. You gots to keep this quiet, hear me girl?"

Couple of weeks later I was in the Quarterdeck after work, working on my third Bud. I still had my painter's pants on. Like most nights I had met Janie at five o'clock and we got a sandwich at Ugi's Subs and then headed to the bar. Janie was sitting at one of the booths with Sean—her boyfriend. Janie was sort of cute. She was thin with red hair and sharp features. She wore tons of makeup. If her nose hadn't been broken I really think she could've been a model. Sean had broken her nose. She told me it was by mistake one night when he'd been drinking.

Anyway, Willa May and Jerome and Matthew were there as usual. Matthew and Willa May were having a fight. Willa May was angry with Matthew because he had quit his job even though Ann was pregnant.

"Why you walked out on that job?" Willa May asked him.

"I ain't talkin to you," he said.

"Your own wife is expectin and you got to pick this time to quit?"

"I couldn't stand workin in that gas station no more," Matthew said. "It was bad enough when old Jackson owned it, but when them Iranians bought it my days was numbered."

"You go back there and ask them for your job back. Maybe they give it to you."

"Woman what you gettin on me for?"

"Cause Ann is a friend of mine," Willa May said. She put her hand on her hip and pointed her finger at him. "Hear me now," she said.

"No," he says, "I ain't listenin to you. You still mad cause Jerome got laid off and you has to work more. That's what this about."

Jerome had been laid off and Willa May was working more hours at the prison. She was a prison guard.

"You ain't nothin but a lazy old cow," Matthew said.

I walked up to the bar beside Willa May to order a round for Janie, Sean and me.

"And you best kept your hands offa this white girl," Willa May said to Matthew. "Ima tell Ann about it."

Matthew stepped around Willa May so he was beside me. "What I tell you about keeping your mouth shut?" he says to me. He was drinking a beer. He had a mean look on his face.

"I didn't tell anyone," I said. "You're just angry. Don't take it out on me."

I thought I heard him growl. "Shut the fuck up," he said and that's when he hit me with his beer bottle—smashed it against my forehead.

I put my hand up to my face and Matthew walked out of the bar. I remember falling down. After that I was half-awake. Janie told me later she had called the police. An ambulance took me to City Hospital. A woman doctor sewed me up—took fifteen stitches. The police came to the hospital and I told them what happened. They asked me would I testify against Matthew and I told them I would.

Six months later there was a trial. Willa May admitted that Matthew had hit me with the bottle. Janie testified too and Matthew was convicted. The judge gave him six months for assault. It wasn't the first time he'd been arrested. I had already moved back home to Carol. I drove up for the trial. Even though I was six months pregnant it wasn't obvious with my body. No one at the trial said anything but of course my momma knew, and soon after that, when I got back from the trial, everyone else in Carol knew too. I had picked up a job in a nursing home twenty miles north of town. I worked up until a week before I had the baby and I went back to work as soon as I could leave the baby home with momma.

Janie and me still keep in touch. I sent her pictures of William—that's what I named him. I figured it wasn't no use telling Matthew about it—what kind of daddy would he make? Janie moved from Roxbury to a better neighborhood in Dorchester. Every once in a while on the news there's a murder near where she lives but Janie tells me it's fine. Fine for her maybe. Me, I realized when I was being sewn up at the hospital that my daddy was right, living in Boston I was like one of those Christians walking into a den of lions. I sometimes think that bottle Matthew hit me with was held by the hand of God. I put that cross my momma gave me back on soon as I got home from the hospital and I been trying to be a good person ever since. I plan to bring my baby up that way too. He's four years old now. At first my daddy didn't want any part of him but momma and me just keep working on daddy and he's coming around. He don't even use the N word no more. Willie ain't black like Matthew was. He's coffee-colored, with freckles. Every night before he goes to sleep, we get right down on our knees and pray together. I mean, who knows? Maybe there is a God.

TWO-FOURTEEN

Sometimes things go from bad to worse. You get up half-asleep and go to work, or don't get up, but lie there, half-asleep. A few years go by and one night you hear the sound of glass breaking. There's someone breaking in, but you're not sure—you could be dreaming. It's stuffy and the quilt slides over your sweaty legs. In the other room, someone you don't know is taking the stereo and TV. You'd stop him only—you're too tired so you lie there. Your wife and kids don't wake up until he's gone—they can't blame it on you.

Weird thing is, that's when things was good. You had a job in a factory, apprentice metal worker, metal worker, someday: master metal worker. You were doing OK, but then they shut the factory down. Said the imports were killing them. Company couldn't afford to keep the place open. You looked for a job for a few months, but the economy was slow. Soon as the economy picked up you'd get back on your feet.

The bar you go to is the same bar you always went to—down the street. Owners—white, have changed twice, don't make no difference to you who owns the damn place. Everyone you know goes there. Murphy, Wilma, Norma, Samantha. You've gone with all three of the girls. Samantha claims she has your kid. You don't believe her and she can't prove it. Can't prove a thing.

The bar was nice once. There was a pool table the owners took out after Jimmy stabbed Frank over a quarter Frank said Jimmy took. And they boarded up the windows, they were broken so many times. Gets real hot in the summer. They open the door to the alley for air but there isn't any.

You drink Bud with Seagrams back. Take the Seagrams straight. Three times and the haze that stays behind your eyes starts to fade. The weight lifter in your head kicks back. Finally you find something Wilma says funny and you hear yourself laugh out loud. "Give me a break," you say and hold your sides. That girl can make you laugh. Make you laugh till your sides ache. Seems her granddad turned one hundred in Jackson, Mississippi. "Whole town turned out to celebrate—rode him around on the fire truck. He had a ball. But, the thing was, he caught a chill, ridin around like that, came down with bronchitis and died ten days later." Wilma hits you on the back and you shake with laughter.

One of these days you'll get back on track. Get up early and have breakfast, not drink all day and into tomorrow. You'll get in shape again—down at the gym one day, road work the next. The way you did as a kid. It can be done. Others done it. The black marks under your eyes will disappear. You'll hold your head up, feel like yourself again. Move back in with Ann and the kids.

Then you hear the voice of that stupid girl—Mary Jane from Pennsylvania. She just moved here and got a job painting houses. She don't even know where she is at. Standin there in your bar, drinking half a dozen beers, gettin all loud with her blue eyes and freckles. She ought to go back down to the farm. Never should have left. They come up here and take the job though. They take the job and the money. You'd like just once to bust someone like her up. You feel your hand close around the neck of your Bud.

Wilma's got hold of your arm.

"Get off me, Wilma," you tell her, but she's trying to warn you about something. You turn around and see Two-fourteen standing with his back to you. Appears to be selecting a song on the jukebox. Still wears that leather hat, black leather jacket and black gloves. Must have kept them in storage while he was away. Four years in Walpole. Two-fourteen was his number. He'll be wanting something you don't have.

Busta Rhymes starts up on the box. Two-fourteen turns and smiles. Cocky smile, even though he lost a couple of teeth. He pushes his hat back on his head. How you ever ran with him you don't know. You shake your head and smile back at him though your nerves are showing. You grind your teeth and you can feel the twitch in your eye. Maybe he can't see that. Maybe it's too small for him to see.

"Let me buy you a drink," you hear yourself say. You sound shaky.

Two-fourteen hits you on the back. "My man," he says. "My main man." He winks at you. "What you got for me, Jack."

You signal the bartender and tell him you want a rum for your friend. Rum on the rocks. Double. You got just about enough for that. You wonder what you'll tell him, how to put it. Then you blurt it out: "I spent it, buddy. I spent some and lost the rest. Three grand goes fast—be surprised."

You and Two-fourteen pulled a little job four years back—before you started at the shop. You needed the money. He got I.D.'d; you didn't. Simple as that, though a number of folks know you were in on it, Murphy, the cop, included. Two-fourteen went up. Seven to ten. Served four. It wasn't his first trip. All you had to do was save his share, he said. You couldn't even do that. If you could have kept that job at the shop things would have been fine, but they shut that place down. Imports were killing them. The Japs and the Germans. You take a hit of your beer.

"You owe me," Two-fourteen says. "Three grand with interest. Four years interest."

"You're right," you say. "I'll get back to you, buddy. Count on it."

"Shit!" Two-fourteen shouts and smashes his drink on the bar. He picks up your beer bottle and breaks the neck off on the bar. He's got you by the collar with the cracked bottle against your cheek. "I'm givin you ten days to come up with that cash, John."

He's gone out the door by the time Eddie, the barkeep, is there to ask, "You all right, John?" He wipes the pieces of glass off the bar. "Wasn't that Two-fourteen?" he asks. "He knows he ain't supposed to come in here."

So that's the way it is. You tell Two-fourteen you'll get him two bills a week until you're square. Six months will pay him double. Where you goin to git that money? You call your old probation officer and he sets you up with the number of a social worker. You leave him a message and three days later who walks in the bar? The social worker. Big government hard at work. He's the one who got you on the government program last time. Big smile on the little man's face.

"What's up, buddy?" you say, smiling too, your hand out to shake.

"Glad to see you're in good spirits, John," he says, "I asked about you at the placement agency a few months ago, but nobody could tell me anything. I knew you had been laid off when the shop closed, but I thought you would find another job."

"Nope—economy is slow."

"Yea, well I made some calls and I got you an interview down at the shipyard. Things down there don't always pan out. They seem to be on the verge of a shutdown every couple of years, but with all the business the President is giving them they ought to be all right as long as he's in."

You're nodding. Taking it very serious but what you don't quite get, what you wonder about is what this dude is after. You got to ask. "Why you go out of your way for me?"

Social worker orders a beer, orders you a new one.

"It's what I do, John," he says.

So you get on at the shipyard doing metal work. Start out at $14.75 an hour, which is just enough to let you pay Two-fourteen, pay the rent for your room, buy groceries and drinks after work. That don't leave nothin for the wife and two kids, but hell, they don't know you are workin. That's one advantage to not livin with them no more. Once the wife finds out though then there just might be trouble. She don't ask for nuthin if you out of work but once you bring in the money then she wants her share. Thing is, a man wants to give it to her and to the kids. They'll be teenagers soon and you want to provide for them but you got to get this Two-fourteen off of you first.

So that's the way it goes for five months. You got maybe three payments left to your main man, and all you been doing is workin and goin home. You stop in at the bar for a pop before you head back to the shack behind the auto body shop where you been living now goin on two years. A little over a month and everything be fine. Be able to breathe again. Maybe even move back home with the wife.

You knock down a second beer with Seagrams back. You got credit now—feelin good really when Wilma shows up. You ain't seen her for ages. Soon as you buy her a drink she wants to know what you're up to and you let slip about the job. Big mistake, she starts in on you right off about Ann and the boys—sayin how now you got a job you ought to be takin care of 'em. What the hell business is it of hers?

"Wilma," you say, "I wants to take care of them but I got somethin else I gots to take care of first."

She ain't in the mood to listen. "Just you get some of that money you been makin into the home fund, brother. I'm tellin you flat out, I got to listen to Ann every day and I ain't goin to be friends with you no more if I have to listen to her complain when I come in here and find you got a job—how long you been workin anyways?"

Wilma pushes you into that girl—Mary Jane who says something stupid like: "Why don't you take it easy, John."

"Don't you tell me what to do," you say, grab the beer bottle and smash it against the side of her ugly, dirty blond, freckled head.

She cries out and drops to her knees where she belongs and you hear Two-fourteen at your back. "Hey pal," he says, "you got some trouble here."

He has a gun in his hand pointed at Eddie who already has his hands up over his head. Everybody stops talkin. There's Busta playing again on the box. He must be Two-fourteen's music man.

"Empty out the register," Two-fourteen says. "Cover my back," he says to you, "cover my back and we square," and you turn around and look at the people in the bar—most a which you know. "Ain't nobody doin nothin," you say to Two-fourteen.

The bartender gives Two-fourteen a pile of bills. Two-fourteen stuffs the money into his pocket.

"Come on," he says.

You move together out onto Washington Street where Two-fourteen has his black Riviera parked and running. He gets in and you get in beside him. Like you have a choice.

CINDY SILK

"Excuse me, Cindy, but these people tell me their food isn't hot," Angelo said.

Cindy stared at the new maître d', puzzled.

"Not hot?" Cindy put her hands on her hips. "It's not supposed to be hot. Tell them that."

"Where do I get these people?" she said to no one in particular. She put her hands on her temples and massaged them. Her throat was so dry she could barely swallow. She looked up and the new maître d' was still standing there. She reached out and grabbed him by the ear. "Did you hear me?" She twisted his ear. "Go," she said, pushing his head away as she released him.

Angelo reeled backwards, an incredulous look on his face.

Cindy turned around, went back upstairs and found David. "I'm going to take a break. Keep an eye on things. Keep everyone moving."

Two hours later, rush over, most of the guests gone, Cindy was talking to Chad, her best-looking waiter. With his thick black hair, square jaw and blue eyes, Chad looked like he could be giving tennis lessons at the country club. Usually she enjoyed talking to him because it gave her the opportunity to stare at him, but now he was irritating her. He stood there, drinking her cognac, at her invitation, telling her that he liked the cheaper one, the Delamain, better than the Vesper, when anyone who knew anything about cognac knew that the Vesper was fabulous. In fact, someone had stolen a bottle of the Vesper which retailed for over a hundred dollars and Cindy thought it might have been Chad. She briefly entertained the notion that he might be right about the Delamain. Then she regained her senses. "No, no," she cut him off, "you don't understand, Chad. It's the quality of the oak that gives the Vesper that woody flavor—what the French call 'raison' from the aging."

"But the Delamain has a nice, fiery quality," Chad said.

"Fiery?" Cindy didn't know why she wasted her time listening to these people. Maybe it wasn't Chad who'd taken the Vesper since he liked the Delamain better. She had owned this restaurant with Meyer for ten years and the waiters were always stealing from her. Here she was actually giving a waiter free cognac, and he didn't even know what was good. Enough was enough. She slammed her empty glass down. "Why don't you punch out, Chad."

She managed a wooden smile. Half the time the waiters forgot to punch out on the time clock. She had told them that she wasn't going to pay them if they didn't punch out yet they still forgot.

She checked her watch—ten o'clock. She had to get out—the restaurant was driving her mad! Meyer wouldn't be done for an hour or two. She could change and go out before he finished in the kitchen. Little Noelle would be asleep. She would have June, the cashier, look in on the kid and baby-sit until she got back. Cindy pictured June's cute face—she would have been attractive if she weren't fifty pounds overweight. Still, she liked June because June did whatever she was told to do.

David, the manager, stopped her on the stairs. He asked her, in that whining, nasal voice of his, if she were leaving.

Cindy looked at his long oval face with his drooping bottom lip and nodded.

"I also wanted to ask whether that California wine came in." David smiled weakly.

"David, why do you have to bother me day and night with these details? You can't do these things yourself? And why is Chad still working here? The busy season is over, right? We no longer need him. Besides, I think he was the one who took the cognac." Cindy drew her hand across her throat. "Get rid of him." Suddenly she remembered that she wasn't sure whether Chad was or wasn't the one stealing the cognac. So why was she telling David to fire him? *Ugh,* there was just too much on her mind.

"Whatever you say, Cindy." David looked at his new Gucci shoes—there were smudges on them. He frowned.

"No," Cindy said, "I didn't get that wine in. Wait a minute," Cindy stopped on the stairs, "I did get it in." She clenched her hands and stomped up the stairs. "Come on," she said. "Follow me."

David followed her up the winding stairs of the Georgian townhouse that Cindy and Meyer had bought five years before and turned into one of the best restaurants in the city. Prior to that they had been in a smaller restaurant around the corner where David had been a waiter. When they moved, she had made David manager of the new place. After Cindy had her child, David had assumed more responsibility. Cindy didn't really like to work so much anymore. Neither did Meyer for that matter. These days Meyer spent only one or two nights a week in the restaurant. The rest of the time he was working on other projects. Most nights, Meyer let the sous-chef, Nick, run things. Meyer had opened a gourmet store on Tremont Street; he had a concession at Tanglewood for music festivals and concerts, and he had a café opening in the fall at the Four Seasons hotel.

Cindy and Meyer have done very well, David was thinking, as he followed Cindy up the stairs. For an Israeli with a liberal arts degree from Dartmouth and no formal training as a chef, Meyer had done incredibly well, and for a girl from Revere with a high school degree and one year of community college, Cindy had done quite well too. All David had to do to keep his job was to jump when Cindy said jump. David already had bought a three-family house in Dorchester and a condo in Boston; he planned to get out of the restaurant business in five years. Until then, he would eat humble pie when he had to.

With a grunt, Cindy picked up and handed to David a case of cabernet sauvignon which had been sitting just outside the door to her apartment. David was walking back down the stairs to the restaurant, struggling with the case of wine, when he heard something crash in the kitchen. He hesitated at the bottom of the second floor. The restaurant was on two floors and the kitchen was on the second. David heard a rasping voice screaming in the kitchen. It was Meyer. David put the case down on the stairs and peeked in the kitchen. Meyer had his broad back to the kitchen door so David sneaked in and hid over by the bread, near the walk-in cooler, to see what was going on.

"What do you call this shit?" Meyer was yelling at one of the young cooks. "Look at this. Look at it. I should rub your face in it. You can't do the simplest goddamn thing. We go over this day after day." Meyer walked over to where the young cook stood at the stove and grabbed the frying pan off the floor. He put it back on the stove and tossed a handful of julienned vegetables into it. He opened the broiler above the stove and put a filet of veal in. "Damn it," he said.

Chad came walking up the service stairs toward David with a tray full of dirty dishes on his shoulder. He was carrying the tray with one hand, and with the other hand, he was eating a tenderloin of lamb that a guest had apparently failed to finish.

"That's it," David said, putting his hands on his hips. "That's the very last straw, Chad."

"Oh, come on, David—everybody eats." Chad took another bite.

"It's against the rules," David said. "This isn't the first time. Besides, she knows you've been stealing cognac. Just get your things and leave."

Up in the apartment, Cindy laid two lines of cocaine on the glass table in front of the television. "So you're addicted," she said to herself, "so what?" Some people were addicted to coffee, some to booze. She liked cocaine. She had managed to stop for the last month of the pregnancy. Besides, she had been eating healthy and going to aerobics classes. Her weight was down and she looked good. She was a nervous wreck, but what could she do?

She had MTV on with the sound off. J. Lo was selling her perfume. After Cindy did the lines she felt better. Much better. It was part of the business, wasn't it? Meyer did it, the waiters, cooks, everybody. Jim, her current flame, would have some tonight. Jim always had good stuff, the bastard. She laughed. Speaking of bastards, she should check on the kid. No, she must be all right or there would have been some noise. Cindy and Meyer weren't married. Cindy didn't care either way. She would have preferred being married, sure, but not being married was fine. She didn't trust Meyer anyway. As if you could trust anyone. She lit up a cigarette, sat down and watched the MTV announcer sticking out her tongue and lewdly licking her lips. Cindy stuck her tongue out back at her.

Chad changed his clothes in the bathroom upstairs on the second floor. *It wasn't David who fired me,* he thought, *it was Cindy.* He took a bottle of Delamain out of his locker and put it in his backpack. He liked the Delamain better than the Vesper.

"Well boys," Chad said as he walked past the waiters on his way out, "I've been fired." He stood in the doorway.

"You'll be back," one of the waiters said.

Chad smiled.

"There's a call for you," the cashier, June, said to him when he got downstairs.

Chad squeezed into June's cubbyhole. She handed Chad the phone.

"Chad, hey, this is Jim. Wondering if I can hook up with you tonight."

"Sure," Chad said, "I'll see you at Division. In fact, I can be there in ten minutes." Chad handed June the phone. "June," he said, "it's been a pleasure."

As he walked out the door of the restaurant Chad was smiling, shaking his head, thinking about Jim and Cindy.

Division was a short distance from the restaurant. Chad nodded at the doorman and walked past a dozen people in line in front of the club. The doorman was new, but he waved Chad in because one of the owners had introduced Chad to him the night before. Chad squeezed into a space near the corner of the semi-circular bar. The bartender put a gin and tonic in front of him. "This is on Jim," the bartender said.

Cindy looked through her closet. She felt as if she were looking through the clothes of a much bigger woman. She pushed the hangers around and knocked a couple of dresses on the floor. "I have plenty to choose from now, ma," she said aloud. She settled on a jumpsuit, but when she got it on and stood in front of the mirror she could see that it was too long. She stood, frozen for a moment, in front of the mirror. She always bought clothes too big. She must have been a bigger person in a former life. She rolled the cuffs up and put on a pair of heels. Her throat still hurt. She went into the kitchen and got a bottle of bourbon out of the cabinet and took a swig.

Downstairs, Meyer was in a good mood because it was busy and he had just sent out the entrees for a party of fifteen. "Oh, I'll tell you something pal," he said to Nick, "I haven't given it to Cindy in a while, but tonight I'm going to stick it right up in there." He grabbed his crotch and growled. "I'm going all the way up in there."

Nick was laughing. "No. No," Nick said. "You can't. She's too small—your wife."

"Oh yeah," Meyer said, "I'm going to split her in half tonight."

Nick was holding his stomach and bending over, he was laughing so hard.

"Well," Meyer said. "Maybe you're right. Maybe I'll give it to the cashier instead."

Meyer left Nick laughing in the kitchen and walked down into the dining room. He leaned over a table, hands clasped behind his back. "How is the food?" he asked, "You like it?"

"Fantastic," the woman said.

"Wonderful," said the man.

"You know I just won an award for culinary excellence," Meyer said, "but I think they picked the wrong guy by mistake." He was smiling.

"You deserve it, really," the man said.

Meyer laughed and moved on to the next table.

Cindy looked out the window. It was quiet on the street. All she had to do was get down the stairs and out. She picked up the phone, dialed the cashier and asked June to check in on the kid every once and awhile. Cindy thought about checking in on Noelle. Maybe later. She hurried down the stairs, slipped outside and walked quickly to the corner of Boylston. She surveyed the long line in front of the bar.

Chad downed his gin and tonic while he scanned the crowd. He caught Jim's eye, and started pushing his way across the room. He edged along the pink walls. All the bars were pink and gray and green. Chad was surprised that he didn't feel as if he had been fired. He felt as if he had been let go, released. He could always find another job. Meanwhile, they were playing the new song by Offspring, one of his favorite groups. Chad edged into the men's room, where Jim was waiting. "What's up?" Chad said.

Jim had to hunch in the men's room, he was so tall. He reminded Chad of David Bowie. Jim acknowledged the resemblance, but insisted he was better-looking. He had on one of those long white flimsy cotton coats popularized by Bowie in a video he'd done with Mick Jagger. The one that practically screamed they'd slept together. "Got anything good?" Jim asked.

"Hot date?" Chad smiled, leaning back against the wall with his hands in his pockets. "Cindy?"

"Keep it quiet," Jim said.

"Oh, everybody knows about it." Chad lit a cigarette. "Yeah," he said, "I've got something. Let me just talk to someone and I'll be back to you in about," he looked at his antique gold watch, "twenty minutes."

"OK," Jim said. He walked out of the men's room to the table he kept reserved. There was a bucket of champagne beside the table and on the table a vase with blood-red roses.

When Cindy got to the door, a doorman she didn't recognize stopped her. He looked about twelve years old. He had a flat top and a diamond stud in one ear.

"Sorry," the doorman said, "you have to wait on line like everyone else."

"You don't understand," Cindy said. "I own the restaurant around the corner. I'm meeting..." She didn't want to say who. "I'm meeting someone here and he's waiting for me inside. No way I'm going to wait on line, I mean in line." Cindy clenched her fists. She hated the expression *on line*. Why did people say that? Did they think they were being original or something? "I don't know who you people think you are," she said. She stamped her foot. "Who do you think you're dealing with? Do you want to keep this job?" She realized she was shouting, but she could barely contain herself. She wanted to rip his little flat top head off. "Do you like working here in Boston? I'll have you blacklisted. I'll make it impossible for you to get work anywhere." She was having difficulty breathing. She felt as if there were something stuck in her throat.

The manager appeared at the door to see what the commotion was. "Cindy," he said, "Come on in. Sorry about that. The kid is new."

"Get rid of him," Cindy said, drawing her finger across her throat. She walked past the manager into the bar. She glanced around the room and spotted the empty table with the roses on it. She needled her way through the crowd.

Chad, who was leaning against the wall, watched Cindy as she sat down. He had just spent five minutes crushing up tabs of Ex-Lax and baby laxative. Chad put his drink down on the bar and edged his way over to the hall that led to the men's room. He found Jim leaning on the cigarette machine. Chad handed him a small, folded packet of paper.

"A hundred?" Jim asked.

Chad nodded and Jim handed Chad a single bill. Jim took the packet and squeezed through the crowd to the reserved table where Cindy was waiting. "Hey," he said and kissed her on the cheek. Jim had one of these little mechanisms—drug paraphernalia that make it possible to do cocaine right at the table—just put it to your nose and discreetly snort. He loaded it and handed it to Cindy, who took a couple of hits and then sipped the champagne—Crystal—Jim's favorite. She preferred the drier Dom Perignon, but she was willing to give in once and awhile. You had to, just to keep them. She knew she could find someone else if she had to, but why bother? Meyer either didn't know or didn't care about her flings. There wasn't anything he could do about it anyway—they weren't married. Cindy wondered if it would make any difference if they were.

"What do you think of the coke?" Jim asked.

"Good I guess. I can't really tell, I'm so wound up. I need to relax."

"Let's go upstairs," Jim said.

Jim kept an apartment above the bar. They went up after they had finished the champagne. They attempted sex but Jim said he was having trouble concentrating. He couldn't seem to get it hard. Cindy finally gave up on him, got up and got dressed. She checked her watch. It was just after two. She'd get home a little early.

She tried to be quiet on the stairs to her apartment just in case Meyer was already asleep. He was always asleep by the time she got home but then she didn't usually get home before four or five.

There wasn't anyone in the living room although the television was still on. Cindy thought she could hear someone exercising. Could Meyer be playing with the kid this late? Well, maybe the kid had woken up. Cindy walked down the hall to the bedroom. The door was half open and Meyer was banging the cashier June. Meyer was on top—the only position he knew. June had her eyes closed. Sweat streaked Meyer's broad back. He was grunting. Cindy hesitated at the door. She could burst in and kill them both with her bare hands. She took off one of her shoes and held it up. She could bury her heel in Meyer's fat head. She saw herself hitting him repeatedly until he lay dead while June screamed hysterically. Just then June turned her head and looked at Cindy.

Cindy took her other heel off, put them in one hand and with her other hand brought her finger to her lips and made a "shhh" face. She backed away and quietly tip-toed down the stairs. At the bottom of the stairs she put her shoes back on.

She walked up a block to Charlie's, a small bar that stayed open after hours. She ordered an Absolut vodka on the rocks and sipped it. She wanted to be mad, but she wasn't mad. She didn't really feel as if she had the right to be mad. She suddenly felt a pain in her stomach. She barely made it to the women's room in time. It seemed as if everything inside her emptied out. She had a dull headache too. That cocaine was not good. For some reason, as she was sitting there, she thought about Chad. Maybe she shouldn't have fired him. He was a good waiter. Maybe he hadn't stolen the cognac. Maybe it was

David. She did not want to fire David. She needed someone like David. She thought of waiters she had fired over the years. She could see their faces but she couldn't remember any of the names. No way could she fire June. She needed June to babysit. Reliable babysitters were worth their weight in gold and June weighed a lot. Cindy laughed and shook her head. She stood up and flushed. She felt dizzy. She'd have to give up the cocaine. She couldn't think straight anymore. She went out to the end of the bar and called Meyer on her cell. He said Hello in a sleepy voice.

"I'm going to be a little late," Cindy said. "I thought I'd give you a call."

"Oh, thanks," Meyer said. He was breathing heavily. "When do you think you'll be home?"

Cindy looked at her watch. She thought about having another drink. "In about ten minutes," she said.

"No rush," Meyer said and hung up.

Cindy sat there with the phone in her hand. Her breath came in gasps. Her throat was so dry she couldn't swallow. If she could just get one more drink, she'd be all right. She glanced up and saw her reflection in the mirror behind the bar. She really did have a small head. She drew her finger across her throat. What if she slit her own throat? Who would care? Jim? Meyer? June? David? Would they cry at her funeral? June would cry. Ma would cry. Tomorrow she'd have David call Chad. She'd unfire him.

She liked Chad actually. Jim was the one who had to go. She grabbed one of her ears and twisted it. She laughed at herself in the mirror. "Right ma?" she said.

BACK-HOE BOB

A narrow paved pathway divides a primordial world of scum: Swamp Thing on the left, Lady of the Lake on the right. Mosquitoes run in mobs, delinquent gangs bent on revenge for the cruel trick reincarnation played on them. Birches, pines and sycamore intermarry. Incest reigns. Damp and fecund, the swamp beckons to empty beer cans, plastic soda bottles, bottle tops. Dragonflies hover and investigate.

I was sitting on a boulder gazing at the pond, sipping a Sierra Nevada Ale and wondering how deep it was. The boulder was left in the middle of the path by one deranged back-hoe operator. Back-hoe Bob digs up boulders and leaves them in the path of absent-minded professors who talk to themselves as they walk around campus, never looking where they are going to trip and fall, scattering reams of notes. At night inebriated students crash and burn while trying to make their way back to the dorms, cursing fate.

I finished my beer and climbed down off the rock. I walked to Jacob's Ladder, a bar just off-campus. It was midnight when I got there, and Back-hoe Bob was waiting. Bob wore his hair long in a ponytail, the black streaked with gray. On this particular night he was clean-shaven, making it hard not to notice two scars on one side of his face that looked like they were made by a jealous owner of a pair of long nails. If Bob stood up straight he'd be over six feet but he never seemed to stand up straight. He was studying the label of his long-necked bottle of Bud when I walked in. He had on black pants and a long-sleeved black shirt.

"Hey, professor," he said, "Beer?" He signaled to the bartender.

"I need Mr. Jose to pick me up," I said.

I love beer, but I love the effect of tequila. It may taste as bitter as the cactus from which it is made but it delivers illumination to the frontal lobe and floods the brain with light. I closed my eyes and winced when I tossed it back.

"How are your students this semester?" asked Bob, cocking his head.

"Worse than ever," I said. "Victims of the self-esteem movement. At least Xers knew they didn't know anything. They were teachable. These kids are convinced they're wonderful as is. What do you think happens when I criticize their papers?"

"What?"

"Can't take it," I said to Bob. "They ignore it. They think I am crazy. They got As all through high school and they never, ever revised. Why start now?"

"Flunk em," Bob said.

"You're right. I should flunk them, but if I do that, then I'll have no students and I'll be out of business." I looked at myself in the mirror. *Who the hell is that?* Beard turning white, long hair unkempt. I shook my head. "What are we up to tonight, Bob?"

"We?" Bob looked at me skeptically

"By the way, I am officially divorced as of today." I downed a shot and raised the bottle of Bud Bob bought me to wash it down. I needed to celebrate or mourn or both. My wife, Kristina, who taught French at Spencer, a women's college just outside Boston, had taken off with her colleague who taught Spanish. This Spanish lover was a little younger than my wife and he had a villa in Spain. Who could blame her? Not me, that's for sure. We didn't have any kids. We had decided not to when we got married for reasons I no longer entirely remember— something to do with not bringing more children into such a world, blah blah blah . . . Anyway, over the years, I think Kristina missed not having kids. I wouldn't be surprised if she and Jorge had a few.

"You want to see if we can hook up with Maria?" Bob asked.

"The woman who used to work in the copy center?"

"You like her, right?" Bob placed a twenty on the bar.

"I'm up for that," I said.

"Go ahead, my car's open. I'll catch up."

As I reached the door I glanced back and saw Bob hand something to Fiona, the bartender, but I couldn't see what it was. Maybe he owed her some money. Or maybe she handed something to him. Now Maria, I remembered talking to Bob about her six months before, when I met her at the Christmas party. Bob seemed to know her pretty well. He introduced me and I danced with her. She had raven black hair that hung halfway down her back and black eyes that radiated heat. She seemed to be aware of her sexiness and capable of playing with it. She always seemed to be smiling. I can still picture the white blouse, short black skirt and black heels. At the time, I thought of asking her to do something—have coffee on her break, anything, just to sit across from her and stare into her eyes, but I was married and wasn't really interested in meeting anyone. Then, sometime between fall and spring semester, she quit and I never saw her again. That's about when my marriage started to go south.

"Yeah, she's a stripper at Candyland." Bob was grinning.

"No." My jaw must have dropped. The thought of seeing Maria peel off her clothes had me going. I could see us dancing together around a fire someplace on some deserted beach—she was stripping just for me. Or I was fighting over her with a gypsy. We each held onto a piece of cloth with one hand and swiped at each other with knives. After I won the fight, Maria and I would make wild love on the beach.

I climbed into Bob's midnight blue 1960 Cadillac. It was in pristine condition. When he got in, he undid a clamp to release the convertible top and I undid the other; then he pushed a button and we watched as the top accordioned back to invite the sky in. It was going to be a good night, I could tell. It was the beginning of my new life.

I looked over at my pal Bob. Bob was a scam artist. Every once in a while there would be a bizarre series of events on campus—some kind of illegal caper—and some kids would get caught and chucked out. One year it was stolen parking stickers: stickers that said Faculty or Administrator or Security or Office of the President. The stickers began appearing on the cars of students and these cars—often old Hondas, Fords and Toyotas—would be parked in prime spaces reserved for the big shots who would find themselves looking for a parking space in the student lots at the edge of campus. Three seniors, all boys, were expelled over it, but everyone knew there had to be someone else behind it. Then there were the fake driver's licenses. Apparently, students would hold giant poster board replicas of Mass. driver's licenses in their hands with squares cut out of the corners for their heads. They would be photographed. The photos would be cropped and given to the students, ready to be put in plastic sleeves at K-Mart. A young woman, a photography major, went down for that one. Another year there was a rash of stolen cars. The culprit was never caught but that year Bob offered me a recent vintage BMW for 5K. He said it had been painted and the numbers changed. I told him I was happy with my old Mustang. "How many miles you got on that thing?" Bob asked. I told him 120,000. "I can fix the odometer for you," he said.

Why the students never turned Bob in, I don't know. Maybe he threatened them. Or maybe he had a go-between—someone who fronted for him. I couldn't prove that Bob was behind these cons but when he'd offered me the BMW, I asked him if he could get me some parking stickers and he just laughed.

Candyland had three bars. Each bar had a raised platform behind it. That's where the girls would take their clothes off and, uh, dance. Some would dance. Some would just kind of slither around. Some were attractive; some were not. Most did not seem to be enjoying themselves. One thin, small-breasted girl who looked about sixteen was shivering and couldn't seem to wait to get dressed again. A stripper who wore a policeman's uniform never smiled and looked as if she held all of us in contempt. I would not like to be handcuffed by her. A third stripper, dressed in a nurse's uniform, had tattoos of snakes on her butt.

She was enjoying herself but seemed to be getting a little old for her job—the snakes were shedding. The crowd was nearly all men. There were a few couples. There were also waitresses in short pleated skirts serving the overpriced drinks. When the dancing girls weren't stripping, they would wander through the bar offering lap dances or raffle tickets or you could buy them a high-priced drink and they would flirt with you.

When Maria first appeared I didn't recognize her. She had her long black hair piled up on her head with pins and the first thing she did up onstage was to take them out and shake her hair loose. She wore a Catholic school girl outfit with a plaid skirt, white blouse and white pumps that required tightrope skills to dance in. I thought she might be shy or awkward. Instead she was confident and sensuous. It made me weak to watch her. She knew what she was doing and she had the men in the audience, including me, in her thrall. She tossed her bra to the crowd and we hooted and hollered. When she exposed and caressed her breasts, we whistled. She pulled her skirt up, turned around in front of Bob and me and gave her ass a slap. Then she turned back and smiled at Bob. Under the skirt, she wore garters that men stuffed with bills. When she finished, I was sweating.

About ten minutes after her act, she came out into the crowd and Bob called her over to the table we were sitting at. "Remember the professor?" he asked from his seat.

"You-all danced together last Christmas. He still talks about it. It was the highlight of his life."

She smiled. She had some of her clothes back on, but her breasts seemed to want to jump out of the lace bra that was holding them back. I tried unsuccessfully to keep my eyes up. I said hello, smiling like a fool.

"Maybe we could drop by your place later," Bob said.

Maria glanced away for a moment and then nodded and smiled. "Sure, why not?"

"For fifty bucks she'll dance on your lap." Bob stood up as she walked away. "Order me one more before they close, would ya Doc? I'll be right back." Bob disappeared into the crowd.

A few minutes later he returned, followed by a tall black woman who had on a pair of bright blue spandex pants and a stretch white tank top. Her pants were hip huggers that went to just below her knees. She wore blue high heels that were the same color. With the heels, she towered over Bob. She had what appeared to be a fake diamond in her belly button.

"This is Cassandra," Bob said. "If it's okay with you, she's coming with us."

"Fine by me," I said. I tried my best to stand up straight. She was well over six feet in her heels. She had her hair pulled back into a tight bun. She had a nose ring, full lips with white lipstick on them and almond-shaped dark eyes. She had shaved her eyebrows and had drawn one higher than the other, which gave her a skeptical look. She leaned back and held her hand out to me.

I didn't know if I was supposed to shake it or kiss her ring. I shook it. It was surprisingly limp.

"This is the professor," Bob said. "We're going back to Maria's, Cassy."

"Y'all gonna fix me up there?" Cassy started sucking her thumb after she asked this.

"You bet," Bob said.

As we left, the lights went on.

Cassandra got into the front seat. I started to climb in back.

"No, honey, come on in here in this big front seat beside me," Cassandra said, patting the blue leather.

I slid in beside her and Bob got in behind the wheel.

"We don't have to go to Maria's," I said.

"Oh, we're goin there all right," Bob said.

That's when I started to get a bad feeling, but I wasn't about to jump ship. I knew I was in another world, one much different from the classrooms and offices and the dinner parties I had been to with my wife. But, hey, I was divorced. I was done with that and all those politically correct academics. This world, the world of Back-hoe Bob, was nothing like that intellectual morass at school. This was the real thing, I told myself, and I was going along for the ride.

Cassandra pulled a small white pipe out of a leather bag she had on her lap. "Mind?" she said to Bob.

"Not as long as the professor joins in," Bob said.

"Gimme your lighter," she said to Bob.

Bob handed a gold lighter to her. She flipped the top, ignited the flame and held it to the little pipe and inhaled.

"Here you go," she said to me, drawing in her breath while she spoke.

I took the pipe and inhaled while she held the flame to it. "Whoah!" I said. I felt like Emily Dickinson—as if the top of my head had come off. But Emily was talking about the effect of reading great poetry. "What is this stuff?" I said when I let my breath out.

"That's crack, baby," Cassandra said. "You ain't never had none?"

I shook my head. "Say," I said a few minutes later when I'd floated back down to the seat, "could I see that pipe?"

Cassandra handed it to me. Her long legs brushed up against mine. I started getting a little excited. She was searching in her bag for something. I wondered what she would do if I were to kiss her neck. It was ebony and smooth as a swan's. My pants suddenly felt tight. I focused on the pipe Cassandra had handed me. It had an elephant carved into the bowl. "Is this ivory?" I asked.

"Yep," Bob said.

"Bobby give me that for my birthday," Cassandra said.

"Isn't ivory illegal?" I said, feeling stupid the minute I said it. In fact I realized that I had had a stupid feeling since I'd taken a hit of the crack. There was a palpable feeling of coming down too. Almost a swoosh, like floating down a wave and landing on the beach. *Where was I anyway?* We were driving. We were on our way to Maria's—that was it. I wondered what my former wife Kristina would think of all this. She would not approve, that's for sure, but hey, she was gone with her Latin lover.

"I got it in trade," Bob said, "from a customer of mine."

Out of the corner of my eye I noticed Cassandra putting Bob's lighter in her bag. She seemed to be a little sneaky about it too. Glancing at him and shoving it in the end of the bag near me. Then she looked at me, smiled and winked as if I was in on it. She put her arm around me and said, "Y'all enjoyin yourself professor?" She reached down between my legs and squeezed. "Oh yeah," she said, "the doctor is in." She laughed.

We slowed down in front of a big, yellow, rambling Victorian and we pulled into a long driveway. A red BMW convertible was parked in it.

"That's Maria's car," Cassy said.

"This is where Maria lives?" I had expected an apartment in a building, not a mansion.

"This is Conroy's place," Bob said. "He's on sabbatical in France and Maria is house-sitting."

Conroy was the chairman of the Business Department. He certainly didn't make enough at the college to support this.

The front door was open and it looked like every light in the house was on. I followed Bob and Cassandra through a couple of high-ceilinged, chandeliered rooms to a huge kitchen with an island in the middle lined with bottles of booze. We stepped through sliding glass doors that opened onto a pool and patio. There was Latin music playing. I saw Maria. She had her back to me but I recognized her long black hair. It fell all the way to a short white skirt.

"Hey, Maria," Bob called and she jumped a little and turned to face us.

"Bobby," she said and smiled. She sauntered over to us and leaned toward Bob as if to kiss him but turned her face so his lips met her cheek instead of her mouth. At the same time she winked at me. That was the second time someone had winked at me that night. What did it mean? We all walked over to the bar. Cassandra leaned up against me. Bob, Cassandra and I all did a shot of tequila then Bob reached over the bar and grabbed three bottles of Bass Ale from an iced sink. He opened them with a bottle opener that was built into the end of the bar and handed one to Cassandra and one to me.

"You seem to know your way around the place," I said.

"I've been here before," he said, smiling.

"Bobby," Cassandra said, putting her hands between his legs, "do you got somethin for me?" I felt a little jealous.

Bob pulled a ball of tin foil out of his pocket and handed it to Cassandra. She unwrapped it and put what I assumed to be crack in the ivory pipe. She reached into her bag and found the gold lighter and held it to the rim of the bowl and inhaled.

Maria handed the pipe to me.

Cassandra's phone sounded and she answered it. "Just a minute," she said.

"It's a John," she said to Bob.

"Two-fifty," Bob said.

"Two-fifty," Cassy said into the phone. "I'll be there in about twenty minutes." She put the phone in her bag. "He's at the Red Roof Inn," she said to Bob.

"I'll run you over," Bob said. "Can you wait here for a little bit?" he said to me. "I'll drop her off and come back."

"Sure, I'm good," I nodded.

As Bob drove off, Maria said to me: "Are you looking for a date, professor?"

"So you both work for Bob?"

"You didn't know? I thought everyone knew."

I pulled my wallet out and looked in it. I had twenty bucks. I showed it to her.

"Don't worry about it," she said, pushing me back onto the couch. She reached down and unzipped my pants and pulled me out. She dropped down onto her knees and put me in her mouth.

About ten minutes later the door opened and Bob walked in. Maria was still hovering over my lap.

"Maria! Did he pay you?" Bob yelled.

"Come on, Bob, it's just a blow job," she said, wiping her hand across her mouth.

I sat up and tucked myself into my pants and buckled my belt and swore under my breath.

"Come on, professor," Bob said, "I'm gonna take you home."

"Right," I said.

On the way I offered to pay Maria or Bob himself the next day.

"That's okay, professor. Let's just say you owe me," Bob smiled.

When Bob dropped me off, I was still a bundle of nerves and wide awake too. So I wandered over to the campus across the street from my apartment and climbed on the boulder beside the swamp. I took out the gold lighter I'd snatched from Cassandra's bag and checked it out. It gleamed in the moonlight. I considered tossing it into the pond, envisioning the Lady of the Lake's hand reaching up to catch it, but I realized that would be foolish. We could all use a little help from the Lady of the Lake or even from Swamp Thing these days, but they do not seem to be around.

OUT WEST

When I climbed down from the Greyhound that Friday in early September of 1975, I felt like John Wayne in *The Searchers* after he had ridden for over a year looking for his niece, Natalie Wood, who had been kidnapped by Indians. It had taken fifty-five hours to get from Boston to Missoula; I was one tired cowboy. I didn't know a soul so I thought I'd check up and down Main Street for a room. I put on my newly acquired white Stetson hat. It cost me $50 at Walker's Riding Apparel in Boston.

I had come to Montana because I had heard it was the last refuge of the once great West; I had always had this strange feeling whenever I watched a Western that out West was where I belonged. Plus, I figured I could pick up a job bartending or doing construction in Missoula because it was a regional town for the western part of the state. I dropped my battered suitcase in front of the front desk of what appeared to be a decent, if somewhat run-down, hotel at the end of Main Street called the Park. I inquired about a room.

"Twenty-one dollars," the clerk said. "We require you pay in advance—have to be careful of transients."

I took the money out. "Will there be any problem if I want to stay another night?" I asked.

The clerk gave me a double take. "Twenty-one dollars a week, son."

A less naive person should have been forewarned, but it was my first trip out West and I reckoned I had chanced upon a bargain. Exhausted, I fell right out in the sagging bed for five solid hours, only to be awakened by the sound of a bass guitar throbbing through the floor. I sat up and brushed the bedbugs off my shirt. I imagined they were a characteristic of Western hotels. I figured I had better ascertain the origin of the bass-heavy rock music which had disturbed my much-needed slumber. I went downstairs to find that the bar was situated right below my room, and where it had been quiet, empty and peaceful that afternoon when I checked in, it was now packed wall to wall with cowboys and Indians.

Anyway, standing there in the Flamingo Bar of the Park Hotel, I was watching a couple dozen men and women dancing with relentless fervor; for a minute I thought it might be a rehearsal for a movie, but no, those were real cowboys with short haircuts and thick mustaches, kerchiefs around their red necks, well worn cowboy hats. Those were real Indians with longish blue-black hair, swarthy complexions, heavy brows and glassy eyes. The band belted out old Rolling Stones songs, loud, off-key and slightly out of tune. I needed to get my bearings so I ducked out of the hotel bar onto Main Street.

Main Street in Missoula ran about half a mile and it was situated between the railroad tracks and the Clark Fork River, in a valley just east of the Rockies. It was really a small town with a few blocks to the north and south of Main—all of them appeared to be lined with bars. I decided to hit a couple and when I did I asked for scotch on the rocks, but there wasn't any, only bourbon which seemed to be served neat, alongside Budweiser or Olympia beer. The entire town appeared to be drunk.

To get myself in sync, I found a liquor store and purchased a half pint of Wild Turkey that I carried back to my room and consumed while watching reruns of *Marshal Dillon* and *Have Gun—Will Travel*. I put on the only cowboy shirt I owned, given to me by my former girlfriend, Janice. It was checkered and had snap buttons in front and at the wrists. I eased myself out the door of my deluxe room and walked tall down the winding stairs in my Tony Lama boots, which I had purchased at Walker's along with the cowboy hat. The boots cost a hundred dollars and were already giving me blisters.

The crowd had swelled and was pushing its way into the lobby. I needled into the bar and ordered a Bud. I was enjoying the beechwood aging when the biggest Indian in the place grabbed me by the arm and said, "Listen cowboy, I'm going to fight you, and when I'm done fighting you, all my friends are going to fight you." He pointed to half a dozen of his mangy looking friends who held up one wall of the Flamingo Bar. They were all laughing. I didn't know whether I was supposed to laugh or not. First I was glad they thought I was a real cowboy, but then I wasn't sure if maybe they knew I wasn't a cowboy and wanted to fight me for that reason. Had I been convinced of their seriousness I might have engaged them just for the sake of being involved in an authentic cowboy and Indian fight.

What I said was, "Hey, that's just what me and my friends are lookin for. Let me go get them and I'll be right back. Don't you go anywhere." Then I left by a side door. I walked around to the front, went upstairs and conked out in my room.

The next day, Saturday, I scouted around some more despite a head-splitting hangover. I caught a baseball game on cable in the hotel bar, then I took a nap. At about eight I pulled myself together, walked down to Wally's Steakhouse and had a decent sirloin for $4.95. I began to think I was getting a feel for life in Missoula. After dinner, I swaggered through a pair of swinging doors into Eddie's Bar and a couple of dudes nodded to me. I ordered an Oly with a bourbon chaser and I settled in to watch the locals play pool. Meanwhile the bartender seemed to be having an argument with a shapely brunette. I entertained thoughts of stepping in on her side the way Wyatt Earp might have, when she reached across the bar, grabbed the bartender by his shirt, and pleaded with him to please take her back. The shirt tore, infuriating the bartender who hesitated not more than one second before hitting the long-haired beauty close-fisted, smack in the mouth. She went into a swoon and dropped to the floor. The bartender leaped over the bar, picked her up under the arms and, pulling her to the swinging doors, her feet dragging along the floor, threw her out like a bag of trash.

Shocked? Me? Well, I was beginning to think I had entered a world somewhat more atavistic than the one I was used to, a world in which folks drank themselves into states of bestiality in which they expressed their rage at will.

I shrugged, shook off my feelings of fear and loathing and placed a quarter on the pool table to indicate my interest in participating in a game. When I turned to go back to the bar I was knocked aside by the woman who had just been thrown out by the bartender. The bartender was still on the customer's side of the bar with his back turned to her. She leaped for him and latched onto one of his legs. "Johnny," she cried, "I can't let you go!" There was blood running from one side of her mouth.

Johnny turned around and dragged her along the floor as if he were in one of those potato sack races where two people each put a leg in the same sack. Johnny's partner had fallen down, but he went on dragging her to the finish line which in this case was the swinging doors where he shook her off and booted her out, once again, into the street. I looked around the room. No one seemed particularly upset. I was beginning to question whether I had come to the right place after all. This did *look* like the West as I had imagined it, but no one was acting the way I expected. I wondered if I shouldn't just hitchhike on back to Boston the next day.

"Who's up?" someone was yelling. "Who's up?"

I shook myself out of my reverie. It was the pool players who were yelling and I was the one who was up. I swayed to the table and racked the balls.

"Got a partner?" one of the guys asked. "You need a partner to play."

I started to protest when a woman stepped forward.

"Cynthia," she said and nodded. "I'll play with you. I like your hat. We'll play for beers!" she called to the two players who held the table.

They nodded in agreement.

I rummaged in my pocket. I only had about five bucks, barely enough to cover one loss. But as I watched Cynthia run the table, I realized I needn't worry. All I had to do was keep my feet. Three games and three beers later Cynthia asked me if I needed a little lift. I nodded and she led me into the office—a back room in the bar. We snorted some of that white stuff that snaps you back to wakefulness and allows you to drink vast quantities of liquor.

Cynthia was good-looking in a tough sort of way. Long brown hair, thirtyish, lean body. I imagined her grandmother a medicine woman for the Sioux. We went back to the pool table where we might have played out the night, but for the entrance of a dude named Milo Miles who, I later learned, had been seeing Cynthia for some time. Milo was skinny, a couple of inches over six feet, with long curly hair and glasses. The last thing I expected from the guy was trouble, and yet he hadn't been in the bar for five minutes when he and Cynthia became involved in a fearsome exchange. They looked at me once or twice, but I didn't seem to be the basis of the argument, which focused on Cynthia's current activities. Milo wanted her home with him. He appeared to be getting his point across pretty well, I thought, when Cynthia smashed an empty bottle of Oly on the side of his head.

A couple of what must have been his friends picked the poor unconscious dude up off the floor and said they would take him to the hospital. Milo was better off in that respect than the woman the bartender had beaten up and thrown out. A look out the swinging doors told me she still lay prone on the sidewalk, nursing her emotional and physical wounds until she had the strength to return to the man who was no doubt her one true love and who remained behind the bar, ragged shirt and all, serving the countless beers Cynthia and I had won. Our bottles of Oly lined the bar as if they had been set up for target practice.

Cynthia suggested we head over to another joint, the Silver Spur, for last call. I was game. I wasn't about to argue. I could see how a simple *I'm kinda tired* might escalate into a full-fledged fight with Cynthia and me crashing from table to table as if we were trapped in a pinball game and me being the damaged goods carted off to Missoula Hospital where I'd be wrapped in a head to toe cast.

Outside, Johnny's girl had regained her feet and was readying herself for another attempt at communicating with Johnny.

"Forget about it, Cheryl," Cynthia said to her.

"I gots to try," Cheryl said and lunged for the doors.

"That lady ought to consider divorce," Cynthia said, tossing me the keys to her car. "You mind driving?"

Her car was a Mustang GT—V8, 318 with a functional air scoop and a supercharger. The tires were 16 inch Generals with mags. Ground clearance—about six inches. The stick was a Hurst five-speed and the wheel ratio was one to one. She told me the Silver Spur was ten miles north of town. We went down Main and took a left on Route 200, where I brought the Boss up to a buck-forty.

We reached the bar by the time Cynthia had finished an unfiltered Camel.

Cynthia informed me that the Silver Spur was a cowboy bar frequented by the ranch hands from the outlying areas in the Western part of the state. When we arrived, many of the guys and gals were dancing slow to the last songs of the night. There were sparkling lights over the big, open dance floor. To one side were wooden tables with wagon wheels painted on them. On the other side were two pool tables. In back of the dance floor was a stage. The music came from a country western band that played those heart-wrenching songs of love and betrayal. The atmosphere seemed friendly, a welcome relief from Eddie's and the Park.

I nodded to myself. This was it—the real thing—what I'd come out here to find with my five hundred in savings. This was the kind of place I could get used to. Maybe they needed some help behind the bar or in the kitchen.

"What we need now," Cynthia said as we approached the bar, "is tequila."

Turned out she was right. Tequila was just the thing. Picked me right up. I looked in the mirror behind the bar. Either it was warped or I was loaded. I pushed my Stetson back on my head. Anyone who didn't know better might think I was one of the boys. I was starting to feel at home when a huge guy with a shaved head insinuated himself between Cynthia and me.

"Shouldn't that be mescal?" he said to Cynthia. He signaled to the bartender. This friend of Cynthia's looked like he played tackle for the L.A. Raiders. He had a hawk-like nose and with the shaved head he looked ferocious from the side, but if he looked directly at you and smiled, which he proceeded to do to me, his eyes were kinda close together and he looked downright friendly. I returned his smile with a weak one of my own that I seemed to be having some trouble maintaining.

The bartender brought a round of mescals. Like tequila, mescal is made from the cactus plant, but mescal has a worm in the bottom of the bottle; the worm is supposed to bring luck to whoever drinks it. The bartender emptied the bottle when he poured our drinks and the worm was in my glass. I wasn't exactly sure whether I would swallow it or not.

Cynthia's big friend laughed, switched glasses with me and downed the firewater in one gulp, catching the worm between his teeth and grinning while he swallowed it.

"Who is this guy?" he asked Cynthia while he stared at me.

It was extremely disconcerting. I pulled my Stetson forward on my head, put my hands in my jeans and stared at my boots. I wondered if I shouldn't have returned to the Park and taken my chances with the Indians. We might have become friends by now, even blood brothers.

"Take off, Piggy," Cynthia said, "go on, beat it."

He smirked and walked over to a group of guys. He motioned to us and they all laughed. Cynthia and I just had time to dance. I leaned into her long black hair and shuffled back and forth. I was beginning to feel sleepy again when the lights went on. We headed with the crowd for the door. When we were under the Exit sign, Piggy appeared. He grabbed for Cynthia, and just as I reached for Piggy's arm in some misguided attempt to dissuade the big fellow from gaining purchase of my ride back to town, someone bumped me from behind. I knocked into Piggy and he must have been off-balance because he tripped over someone else and went sprawling backwards into a table where a few cowboys were finishing off their last drinks. Piggy split the table in half and before he could regain his feet the three cowboys who had been sitting there jumped him. I didn't quite know what to do. I tried to pull one of the cowboys off but he was much bigger than me and before I got him halfway off, I collapsed on top of him and fell into the pile. There was a whole lot of grunting goin on down there. We rolled in a pile in what might have been misconstrued as a group hug by someone who didn't know what the nature of our affiliation happened to be. I got in a few punches although I've no idea whom I hit. Finally I managed to shimmy out of the pile and get to my unsteady feet. As I left, they were flailing away blindly at one another with their fists.

"Don't worry about Piggy," Cynthia said in the parking lot. She got in on the driver's side and pushed open the passenger door for me. I got in, closed the door and handed her the keys. I was in no shape to drive. On the way back to her place in town, she told me she had been married to Piggy for two and a half years. They had lived, she said, on a few acres in a town called Wisdom. One day, Cynthia was butchering a cow when Piggy was dumb enough to get her into a heated argument about who was boss.

"He should have known better than to hit me when I had that knife in my hand," Cynthia said. "I gave it to him in the side—right up to the handle. He was lucky I was using the small knife at the time. I brought him to the hospital where they stitched him up and kept him overnight. I moved out while he was in the hospital." Cynthia glanced over at me. "I should have killed the son of a bitch."

When Cynthia and I finally got to her place we attempted sex. She was a fine looking woman and you must believe me when I tell you I wanted in the worst way to make that gal happy. But with all the beer and tequila and coke, the trouble at Eddie's, the fight at the Star, and the story of Piggy, I couldn't quite get up for it. I asked Cynthia if she minded if we just went to sleep.

To my great relief, Cynthia said, "Sure, I'm kinda tuckered out myself."

"Say cowboy," Cynthia said a few minutes later, "where's that nice hat you had on?"

I put my hand on my head. "Damn," I said, "I must have lost it at the Silver Spur."

"I'll run you out there tomorrow," Cynthia said. "It'll be there. Unless Piggy took it. He's just ornery enough. By the way, where are you staying?"

I told her I had a room at the Park.

"The Park? The Park Hotel?" Cynthia put her hand on my knee. "Are you just visitin or are you lookin for work?"

I told her I was lookin for a job bartending or in construction.

"Hell," she said, "you can stay here until you find a place. Eddie is lookin for a day bartender."

"Eddie?"

"Yeah, you know, Cheryl's old man?"

I nodded and looked down at my knuckles which were raw and swollen. I saw myself working the day shift at Eddie's, pulling Cheryl and Eddie apart, propping Milo Miles up against the bar after he had the temerity to engage in yet another argument with Cynthia; then I saw myself getting married to Cynthia with everyone from Eddie's bar at the ceremony and right after we were pronounced man and wife we were accosted on the steps of the church by Piggy and I had to shoot it out with him right there on

Main Street. Luckily I was wearing a Colt .45 and like Matt Dillon, my aim was true.

I shook my head. Sitting there on Cynthia's bed in Missoula, Montana, I felt kind of like Alan Ladd just before he strapped on his gun to go after Jack Palance in *Shane*. I hesitated.

MIND AND BODY

Those days I believed in Body over Mind. I believed Mind followed Body because I knew matter could think. I was a cook in this little hotel/restaurant in Missoula, Montana. The manager put me up in a room till I could find my own place. I had stopped in Missoula, a mill town on I-90, to wash the road off, eat, conk flat out on a bed. I had a couple hundred to get me to the coast but when I saw the hand-written sign for a cook, five bucks per with room and board, I figured I'd work for a while, see what I could pocket. The place—a counter and tables—six rooms upstairs—was open at 6 a.m. and closed down after dinner at night. They had a chef for lunch and dinner; they wanted me to do breakfast and prep.

The manager, Mike, showed me the set-up, my room, told me what my hours and duties were. I could see he lifted weights and must've played football because his body was a series of blocks set atop one another and the top block was his head. His square face had a soft look to it though, no scars on his skin, but a broken nose probably from ball, and though he was young, his hair was thin on top. He shook my hand and his fingers were limp. I knew I could work with him. He told me he split time with his wife who played hostess.

Working the grill for breakfast is a piece of cake—eggs, bacon, ham, and potatoes you parboil, fry and pile in a corner. There are two drawbacks to fryin—heat and grease. The heat comes from the grill and the busier it is, the hotter it gets. The grease comes from the bacon and ham and sausage and the oil you put on the grill and scrape off whenever you can with the spatula. Trouble is, it gets busy and hot, you forget to clean the grill and the grease starts poppin' till you're wiping it off your brow and into your hair. It forms a sheen on your face and fills your pores so your skin can't breathe and hope gets locked in your body.

Sharon, the wife, was on in the mornings with me. When I first saw her I didn't think much—she seemed a little overweight, kind of plain looking, cat green eyes set too close together. I was relieved because I have this problem with women where I get between them and their men. I swear I don't know what it is. Well, what it is, I guess I like the action. I like to magnify the conflict and watch the drama because otherwise it's a goddamn bore. Life, I mean. So I was relieved, sort of—she was not my type. But then, the days went by, soon it was October when the sky turns to slate in Montana and drops down on your shoulders. The sameness of the days made me notice little things, like she was working herself for me, turning herself out—heels in the morning—skirts with buttons she would undo up to the thigh, see-through blouses, plenty of make-up and lipstick caked like blood, hair pulled away from her face. I began to see she was hotter than I first thought.

One afternoon she knocks on my door, foxy in her slit skirt. I'm out of the shower on my way to take my nap—towel round my waist. She tells me she has fresh linens for me—holds the sheets to her breasts. She squeezes past me into my room and drops them on the bed. So when she turns around, I do what she wants—pull her to me, kiss her like it matters. She backs me right into the bathroom beside my bed. I'm a little confused, but I pull her skirt up anyway and lift her up on the edge of the sink. She pulls her panties to one side with one hand and reaches for me with the other—yanks off the towel and pulls me to her by my dick. She's ready and wet. "Give it to me, Roy, fuck me," she says and I lift her off the sink and hold her, big as she is, just the way I like them. She is full of filthy talk. I fuck her till I come and remain hard; she comes and I come again. And for that brief moment we erase that gray Montana sky and block the rancid smell of the saw mill and, with the odor of sweat and sex, fade into each other.

Those days I trusted my body to tell me what was right. I believed that words could lie, looks were put on and actions were deceptive. Our bodies, I thought, were all we had. I trusted her smell and the coarse texture of her skin, the blond hair between her legs, the feel of her tongue pushing against mine.

Things went on between me and her for months before Mike finally opened his eyes and smelled the java. I literally had to console the big guy; he wept like a baby in my arms. He told me he didn't deserve her and he just wanted her to be happy. It was pathetic. The next day, Sharon and I took the bus to Seattle.

We rented a house on this island in the Sound—Bainbridge Island. Both of us worked in a bar in the city. I was a bartender and she was a waitress. We did this for almost a year and for a while, for months, it was good between us—just like it was that first day in my room in Missoula, Montana. But slowly what was between us smeared like lipstick and wore off. She caught me with a waitress in the coat-check room. I caught her with two bartenders in a Cadillac in the parking lot. I pulled one of them out of the car and smashed his head through the side window. The other one popped open the glove compartment, pulled out a long-necked .22 and shot me in the face. Call me lucky, the bullet went through my cheek and tore a hole in my ear.

I remember waking up in the hospital with Sharon holding my hand. We made up and stayed together for about a month, but we were just pretending—it was no good. One day I came home and found a note. She had taken the bus back to Missoula. That's when I began to see I couldn't trust my body any more.

It took many years of bad experiences to change. Now, I put my trust in Mind. I learned to think it through because the body can betray you like a brother. Though matter can think, we can outthink it. And that's what I aim to tell the parole board next month. And this time, I believe they'll set me free.

ACKNOWLEDGMENTS

Some of these stories have appeared in the following publications: "Cindy Silk," *Per Contra* (Summer 2016); "Quality Time," *Hobart* (June 21, 2015); "Luck," *Per Contra* 26 (Winter 2012); "The Orchard," *Per Contra* (Summer 2012); "Body Surfing," *Per Contra* 19 (2010); "A Rare Night Out," *Per Contra* 15 (2009); "Mind and Body," *Hobart* (October 1, 2008); "Getting in Trouble," *Bellevue Literary Review* 7:2 (Fall 2007); "The Fall of Iran," *Cream City Review* 30:2 (Fall 2006); "Out West," *The North American Review* 284:3-4 (May/August 1999); "Two-fourteen," *Princeton Arts Review* IV:1 (Autumn 1999); "Narcissus," *Confrontation* 66/67 (Fall 1998/Winter 1999).

ABOUT THE AUTHOR

ED MEEK is a freelance writer and the author of three books of poetry: *Flying, What We Love,* and *Spy Pond.* His work has appeared in magazines, journals and newspapers, including *The Paris Review, The Sun,* the *North American Review,* and *The Boston Globe.* He is living the dream with his wife in Somerville and Wellfleet.